RANDOM ENCOUNTER

All characters are fictional.
Any similarity to any actual person is purely coincidental.

A catalogue record for this book is available from the British Library

ISBN 978-178035-676-1

First published 2013 by
FASTPRINT PUBLISHING
Peterborough, England.

Random Encounter

– KATHLEEN STEELE –

An environmentally friendly book printed and bound in England by
www.printondemand-worldwide.com

Mixed Sources
Product group from well-managed forests, and other controlled sources
FSC www.fsc.org Cert no. TT-COC-002641
© 1996 Forest Stewardship Council

PEFC Certified
This product is from sustainably managed forests and controlled sources
PEFC
PEFC/16-33-415
www.pefc.org

This book is made entirely of chain-of-custody materials

Chapter One

Dusk was already approaching and the sun rapidly tiring of the day was now tracing its way towards the Western Shores but Jayne Taylor stubbornly held onto the rails that separated the promenade from the shore and gazed transfixed out across the ocean which now appeared to have turned into an uninviting grey in its colouration. With the evening fast approaching folk were already beginning to scurry homeward bound where the night time cosy glow of a fire awaited them as well as offering its warmth against the evening chill, but Jayne Taylor did not move for in truth she herself was waiting there until she spotted the lights of the cross channel steamer heading towards the port. Neither could it be said that folk took too much notice of this figure dressed in leathers, that was until she undid her helmet and allowed the breeze to ruffle her golden locks, which once released from their confines flowed freely so that one could no longer believe this figure to be that of any man.

The task that had brought her to these parts was really quite simple for Jayne was now a courier waiting for the parcel that was about to come on that ferry boat from across the Channel, hence the leathers which she had managed to rescue from the box left by her brother when he had been drafted overseas. Not that she had always been a courier, oh no, for Jayne had once held a good position in a firm which folk seldom associated with liquidation. But the recession that was hitting most of mainland Europe had also hit England hard, and the result was the Jayne had soon found herself without employ. Nor in the current climate were other jobs so readily available, that indeed was the reason why she had taken the job as a courier and what was more to the point this was her first mission; to meet the ferry when it came into port, collect a parcel from one of the seamen and then deliver this to the address she currently held in her pocket.

Perhaps this was not a job that Jayne Taylor would have taken by choice for to her mind couriers appeared to be a race set apart, men on fast motorcycles who dodged the traffic to reach their destination and Jayne had no motorbike of her own although in the past she had gained some experience of the art of driving one when her brother had been at home, neither did she travel fast, but this unfortunately was the only employ that was available and therefore not really knowing what to expect she had taken the job quite readily when it meant keeping the wolves from the door. In truth she supposed she should have taken her family into her confidence before embarking upon such a mission. Perhaps they had already missed her and wondered where she had got to.

But then Jayne had been determined to accept no charity especially where Simon was concerned for the man's answer to everything had been to dip into his back pocket to supply her with any funds she needed whilst at the same time reminding her in his own indomitable way that money did not grow on trees and therefore it was high time she learnt to live within her means and to cosset her employ as well as any employer who was willing to take her on.

That of course was the way in which he anticipated his future wife would operate but then cloistered in his own world of banking and finance Simon had little idea of how the rest of the country managed to survive. Her parents also would have been most upset if they had realised what she had resorted to do, but then financially they were in no position to help her out and furthermore she would never have expected them to have done so.

Therefore this courier's job which paid handsomely for her services had seemed to be the answer to her problems. Not that she had ever worked as a courier before but at the time they had appeared desperate to get hold of someone who was willing to collect this consignment from the docks and deliver the same to the address they had furnished. Consequently enthralled with the idea of having obtained at least some employ Jayne had never enquired as to the contents of this consignment, perhaps she did not consider this to be any of her business. Instead she had equipped herself with her brother Robert's riding gear and also his machine, praying at the same time that she would do neither any harm!

Now looking out across the ocean in what was now semi darkness she made out the lights of that vessel that was now making its approaches to the port and as pleasant as it had been gracing the promenade and painting it with her thoughts, the approaching presence of this craft made her aware that now she had to shift her position and move in the direction of the dock gates where she was supposed to be handed the consignment by one of the crew.

Hers was not the role of gracing the ship itself with her presence for her place had been hallmarked as being outside of the dock gates therefore even as she revved up her bike she knew that she still had some time before the boat docked and its contents had been passed through the security of that place. Still she supposed that riding the bike itself was a new venture. Of course she had ridden in the past when her brother had taken to riding a bike before he joined the army and she did have a license that allowed her to take this thing out onto the Queen's highway, that has been part of the deal for her employ, that she had access to a bike herself and as her brother Robert's was presently gathering dust in the garden shed along with his leathers she did not think he would mind if she exercised the thing for him.

Thus it had taken her most of the day to travel from her home town to this place on the South coast of the country and maybe whilst she was here she would have dearly have liked to have seen some more of the place, but that was not written in her contract for as a courier she had been employed to pay the place a flying visit only simply to collect and deliver the consignment she had been allotted.

The cars were already alighting from the ferry when she finally reached the port and for a brief second Jayne actually wondered if she had arrived late. What she had not realised was that the crew departed the ship after everyone else had gone ashore, a brief visit before they were due to start loading up their cargo again for the return journey, but after what appeared to be a long time the man she was waiting for eventually appeared signifying that he had just passed through security.

Seeing him standing there with the parcel in his hand, Jayne rapidly searched for her own papers of authenticity cussing herself that she had not got them handy. Eventually found however she made to approach the crewman who by this time was beginning to look a little frustrated at what he saw as a delay and appeared to be anxious himself to be able to report back and resume his duties.

Therefore upon seeing her documentation he handed the parcel over to her with something of a grunt. Perhaps he himself was surprised to see a woman there to collect it instead of some man but then he said nothing to that effect because of the time factor for upon giving it to her the sailor made a rapid exit and Jayne was left to fit this object into her panniers, and looking up after doing this she saw that the seaman had gone and the only folk remaining where those passengers who themselves were now making their way into the Ferry Terminal ready for the next sailing.

Jayne reached for her road map of the area. Well Canterbury she supposed, that being the destination where she was supposed to deliver the box to, was not all that far distant and the evening was not so late as to prevent her from completing the task she had been hired to do that same evening. At least she supposed that by doing so she would feel some mark of achievement on this her first venture in this field. Therefore it now became a simple matter to release the bike from its stand and start to rev up the machine.

Perhaps it was the noise of that engine that made her unaware of the car which had decided to stop close by her present position. For the first time she realised that it was there was when she spotted two police officers confronting her and bidding her to stop in her attempts to start the bike. Feeling a little mesmerised as to their presence and wondering if she had infringed some parking rule, Jayne nevertheless did as she was bid although what was to follow was by no means included on her agenda and perhaps she rashly decided that these people wished only to check her credentials for driving the thing..

"Miss Taylor, we have reason to believe that you have just taken delivery of a box from off the ferry that has recently arrived in the port?"

Jayne found it difficult to nod in response. To begin with she had no idea how these messengers of the law actually knew her name let alone her business in these parts, and secondly her helmet prevented her from moving her head in the appropriate manner.

"In that case could we please see this box you recently took delivery of?"

Jayne decided that this whole episode was rather silly. It was only a small box so there was little hope she was carrying contraband ashore in it. Nevertheless having no axe to grind and wanting to finish with this matter so that she might be able to carry on to Canterbury before the hour grew too late, she rescued the same from her pannier and handed it over to the policeman whilst releasing her own head from its constrictions. Much to her surprise however the man made no attempt to open it but instead tucked it deftly under his arm.

"I am afraid that we must ask you to accompany us to the station Miss Taylor!" The order came like some kind of indictment and Jayne swallowed hard. This was not on her itinerary for if she was delayed in this manner then her chances of reaching Canterbury before nightfall would rapidly diminish.

"But whatever for? I need to get to Canterbury tonight in order to deliver the parcel for that is my charge!"

"I am afraid that perhaps you do not understand the gravity of this situation Miss. I think it might be better if you agree to come quietly with us!" He motioned towards the waiting police car and Jayne now regarded her bike with some trepidation.

"Lock it up and I will instruct one of my men to collect it!" The officer had obviously guessed her thoughts and what was more stood over her while she completed this task before he made to escort her back to the police car where he opened the back door to enable her to get inside.

In truth Jayne wanted to make a fuss and to insist that the delivery of such a parcel was merely her job but something in the seriousness of the officer's face made her refrain from issuing forth a mouth of tyranny. All right, so the men had made a mistake but she felt sure the matter would soon be cleared up once they arrived at the police station and then she would be free to carry on with the task that had been given to her and perhaps if she remained silent now then the proceedings whatever they consisted of would pass a little more smoothly.

* * *

Such thoughts of completing her task however appeared to be futile for she seemed to have been in that room accompanied only by a woman police officer, who was conspicuous in her silence, for what seemed to be positively ages before the man finally re-appeared, by which time Jayne had completely lost any hope she had of making Canterbury that day.

"Detective Inspector Bennett would like to have a word with you Miss!" It was the officer whom she had met earlier who was the one who made the introductions and once having made them he immediately disappeared.

The man, Detective Inspector Bennett or whoever he liked to call himself, was not someone she had seen before yet under his arm he carried the incriminating box and placed it on the table between them.

"I suppose you are aware Miss Taylor of what this box contains?" There was not a smile on his face as he stared at her awaiting her reply with wide blue eyes that she swore must be able to see through anything.

Jayne shook her head. After all it had been none of her business as to what the parcel contained. Her brief had simply been to collect it from the docks and to deliver the same to the address in Canterbury to which the box was labelled. "Well it is only a small box therefore I cannot see that it contains very much apart from perhaps someone's souvenirs perhaps left on the continent!" In truth by this time Jayne wasn't particularly interested in what the box contained she simply wanted to be finished with the whole issue.

"Perhaps you had better open it Miss Taylor!" The Inspector pushed the box across the table in her direction. Immediately she could see that it had already been opened for the fasteners had been loosened.

"I'm not really interested in the contents and anyway as you obviously already know for yourself what is inside of it then perhaps you had better tell me!" Jayne began to feel her hackles beginning to rise. This was all a complete waste of time and if things carried on in this manner then she most definitely would not be able to reach Canterbury at a reasonable time that day.

"Perhaps we had better take a look!" With the box between them the man slowly began to reveal its contents. Jayne took one look before responding in disgust.

"Why it looks like a lot of old junk to me!" In response her opposite number looked at her as if he could not believe what she had said. "Anyway it can't be worth a lot for it is such a small box. In actual fact I wondered why they needed a courier to deliver this for I would have thought the postal service would have done just as well!"

"Miss Taylor, this happens to be a consignment of class A drugs with a street value of quite a great deal of money!"

"Oh is that what it is?" Jayne looked again. She had never seen drugs like this before indeed she was not acquainted with any type of drug, and then she realised that they were most probably illegal. "So I presume they are not a legal commodity?"

"Most certainly they are not! Your naivety does you credit Miss Taylor even if it is quite unbelievable!"

"Look all I was employed to do was to take the parcel I received from a seaman and transport it to a certain address in Canterbury. Nobody enlightened me on the contents of the parcel and indeed why should they?"

"The seaman that you say handed you the parcel does not appear to exist according to the ferry service personnel rota. Therefore we would like to know where exactly did you obtain this parcel from."

"I have already told you. I was handed the parcel by someone in a seaman's uniform who appeared anxious to get back to the ship and no doubt his duties!"

"That of course is quite impossible for any seaman leaving the ship would have had to have passed through security. I doubt very much that anyone could have passed drugs through there, especially as the sniffer dogs happened to be in action and would have soon located the drugs for that is why they are employed at the ports:

But the name on this parcel; might I ask who the recipient of this consignment was to be?"

"As you already have the name and address of this person then you are as wise as what I am. I have no connection with this person, I was merely told to deliver the parcel to this man at the same address and that was my intention when your friends apprehended me!"

"Ah!" The man seemed to ponder a little. "Perhaps it might be to our advantage if we paid a visit to this Mr Luc Mathieu and hear what he has to say about the matter!" He still seemed to be thoughtful but seeing Jayne's expression he hastened to add. "Mr Luc Mathieu is the person to whom you say you were supposed to deliver this parcel to. It has his name and address on the label, surely you must have noticed that Miss Taylor!" The Inspector spoke to her almost as if he was addressing some child and Jayne took exception to his tone.

"I only go by the name of the person in my delivery book to whom this parcel is destined for. Yet on this occasion you are right, the name of the person is a Mr Luc Mathieu of Priory Manor in Canterbury! Not I insist that I know anything about this person for I was simply completing the job which had been allotted to me!"

"Then I suggest we visit him in the morning, the hour being now far too late for us to make the journey and arrive at a reasonable time this evening. I have never found people inclined to be co-operative if one rouses them from their bed!" Perhaps the Detective Inspector had now decided that he was wasting his time arguing with this girl and was seeking a solution to the matter.

"You say we Inspector?"

"Of course, you will be accompanied in the police car in making this visit. In the meantime I suggest you accept our hospitality here at the station!"

"Then you are arresting me, on what charge please?"

"You have not been arrested at the moment Miss Taylor. In fact I do not believe you have yet been cautioned. Shall we say that you are helping us with our enquiries?"

"What about my bike?" It seemed to be a silly question she supposed but then it did belong to her brother.

"It is being taken care of Miss Taylor. It seems to be a rather large bike for a girl like you to be riding?"

"I have got a license, although the bike actually belongs to my brother who can hardly use it when he is serving with the army abroad at the moment!"

"Understood Miss Taylor, but then you can rest assured that it will be returned in a fit condition for you to hand it back to him. And now I am sure that Policewoman Smithers will attend to your immediate needs and we will meet up again in the morning when no doubt we will be able to resume our conversation after meeting Mr Luc Matthieu and hearing what he has to say about the matter!" With that the Detective Inspector possibly thinking he had exhausted all avenues for that evening left the room leaving her to the tender mercies of the Policewoman.

★ ★ ★

It was hard to sleep on the mattress that was allotted to her, which Jayne was sure had seen better days and thus simply waiting for the first tendrils of the dawn to appear seemed to take an interminably long time. She supposed she was fortunate in a sense that she was allowed the use of a proper bathroom as there appeared to be no other prisoners in residence at the time and at least this factor was far better than having to use a bucket located somewhere in a dusty corner of that room. During the night time hours a silence appeared to have descended over the place and at first she wondered if the station had all been shut up and abandoned for the night until she realised that there would probably be at least one officer in the outer office but whether the man was snoozing or not she could not tell for the whole place seemed to be as quiet as the grave.

At least her predicament allowed her the time to think as to how she had managed to land herself in this unenviable situation. She could just imagine Simon regarding her down his nose at the moment for bankers seldom wanted to have anything to do with folk who apparently had got themselves on the wrong side of the law and no doubt her own parents would gasp in disbelief and consider that the job she had found for herself was a grave error of judgement on her part. She thought of her current employers, the police had asked about them but upon her response they had obviously checked and appeared to be quite happy over that situation. The fact of the matter was, where had that parcel come from and why had it been addressed to the same person as her own was supposed to be going? That question of course appears to be insolvable and what was more the police appeared to have her marked out for something she had not done. Furthermore whatever anybody said she knew full well that it was a seaman from off the ferry boat who had handed her that parcel as she had expected and there was little point in saying that such a man did not exist.

Still toying matters over in her head brought her no nearer to find a solution and dawn had finally broke when Jayne fell into an exhaustive sleep. The next thing she knew was when the same policewoman was back this time bearing her some breakfast. Jayne was sure she must have a secret door into the place for Policewoman Smithers did not appear to enter by any conventional method. Still Jayne had barely time to eat the toast let alone be tempted by the cereals when she became aware of the loud noise of the Detective Inspector entering the building and she sighed for by the noise he made this man had certainly not passed an uncomfortable night like she had herself!

"As soon as you are ready Miss Taylor we will be on our way!" She noticed that again he had the other officer in tow. Perhaps it was indeed a fact that the two of them could not move without each other. Jayne looked at the remains of her toast and suddenly decided she was not hungry something her mother would have played pop about if she had known for her mother always insisted that you never went anywhere without first having your breakfast. There again this was hardly anywhere and perhaps the sooner they got the matter over with then the sooner these officials would begin to realise their mistake and let her go!

Thus still feeling a little bedraggled Jayne allowed herself to be escorted from that building. Outside the weather had apparently taken a turn for the worse and Jayne shivered as the cold breeze now whipped across her face whilst the cloudy conditions most definitely held the promise of rain within them. She supposed that leathers were hardly the most appropriate garment for wearing for this form of road travel, but now it appeared that she was stuck with them so that even if during the journey she did begin to get rather warm on that seat, especially considering the driver had decided to turn the heating on in the vehicle, this was something which she simply had to put up with. All she prayed was that the journey would not last for too long!

★ ★ ★

The room like all the others in that building was spacious and situated as it was facing south it should have proved to be a delight with the sun shining in through those French windows. Today however there was no sun and the flimsy daylight reflecting on those heavy damask furnishings seemed to be all but suffocated beneath the dark fabric. Neither could it be said that the occupants of the room at that time, who were all seated around that large oval mahogany table, breathed any inflection of lightness to that gathering. For they were all sombre faced and whilst obviously bored at having been summoned to attend this meeting nevertheless they were also waiting with baited breath for the words of one man who held in front of him the pages of a last will and testament which he seemed determined to read out word by word in a slow monotonous voice.

Neither could it be said that any of the faces attending that meeting seemed to awaken from their sullen mood during that reading for the contents they had obviously been eagerly awaited did not please them upon their hearing and as the voice of this person droned on eyes became fixed in one man's direction, eyes which held within them sparks of anger when they had not heard the words which they wanted.

Luc Mathieu took a long sip of water from the glass in front of him as if to moisten his lips which the fire from the other folk's eyes appeared to have dried and parched. There were other glasses and decanters on the table but no one else appeared to want to avail themselves of them but instead they fixed their eyes upon this one individual as if hoping the water he sipped would by some means poison him for to their eyes this was an interloper, one who had entered the family unannounced and who now was seeking to deprive them of the assets which they considered to be rightfully theirs.

Perhaps the main reason for the venom that was now extracted was that Luc the son of the disgraced daughter of the old Lord, disgraced because the woman had the audacity to marry a Frenchman, was the only living descendant in the true line of succession and thus cousins and other family members who had supported the family in years past, mainly for their own reasons, were now excluded. Indeed the first time these so-called relatives had clapped eyes on the man they termed as an interloper was when he had attended the Lord's funeral, although why he had bothered to leave his French home to attend that was beyond the conjecture of many of those who were present. He had made the excuse as he had walked behind the coffin drawn through the parish to the local church where his ancestors were buried, and which had been drawn by the ceremonial black horses, that his mother was far too ill to attend and then immediately after the funeral he had returned to France not to return until it was the day for the reading of the will.

It was the ringing of that bell which suddenly appeared to furnish the assembly with some symphonic rendering to their fit of melancholia; melancholia not so much induced by the departure of that relative but rather on the substance of those papers which the legal man had laid out in front of them before diligently reading out the wishes of the deceased. Moreover the sound was soon to be followed by the entrance of the faithful old butler who could with patience merely amble to deliver his message due to the creeping arthritis brought about by the aging process. In actual fact Jervis the butler had been brought out of retirement for that day simply because the family did not feel it fitting for the housekeeper, who happened to be a woman to hold that position in distinguished company. Moreover halting any further conversation Jervis then gallantly struggled to where Luc was currently seated and whispered something in the man's ear.

This appeared to be a signal for the young pretender to rise and excusing himself from the gathering he made over to the door leaving the butler to further incite those who were left by throwing up his arms in abject horror before painfully making to follow his new master. Such an action now appeared to be a signal for others gathered in that room to rise if only to move their bodies in a better position in an attempt to hear what was happening.

Although the butler had whispered the name of police in Luc Mathieu's ear, that gent was probably more confused than anyone else as to why such members of the law force had decided in their infinite wisdom to pay him a visit and thus he reached the front door questioningly perhaps surmising that these officers had after all come to the wrong place.

"Mr Luc Mathieu?" His theory of the police having come to the wrong place was quickly dispelled as the spokesman from that group spoke upon seeing him.

"Yes?" Perhaps Luc's eyes were now fixed on the parcel which one of the officers held almost as if it was some lethal object.

"May we come in?" The officer obviously had no intention of conducting any business on the doorstep and considering the man already had his foot in the door Luc could hardly refuse. Therefore he nodded and motioned towards the door of a further room whilst at the same time regretting the fact that he had not required the housekeeper to remove the dust covers off the furniture before Jervis had arrived, but then Mrs Bentham seemed to have a fixation about such things if rooms were not in use. Standing aside to let them pass by him into this room Luc did wonder about one of his uninvited guests, a girl apparently still clad in riding leathers, a dress code that gave lie to her flowing locks that were quite unconstrained.

"This parcel addressed to you at this address, where you expecting it?" The leader of the policemen made no bones about brandishing the article once they were all inside of that room and the door had been closed, much to the consternation of the rest of the party who now found it difficult to hear what was going on.

"Why yes I was!" Luc glanced at his name neatly displayed on the label of the parcel that had now been hastily re-wrapped. "But I was expecting it to come by courier service!" Luc glanced again at the girl. Dressed in her leathers he wondered whether she could have been the one who was supposed to have delivered it to him?

"Might I ask what you expect to find inside of this parcel Mr Mathieu?" By this time Luc gleaned an almost sardonic tone in the officer's voice. "Perhaps I should introduce myself, I am Detective Inspector Bennett!" Maybe he thought that this introduction would give him some credence in front of the young man but by this time Luc was beginning to feel a little mesmerised.

"Of course you may ask. I am actually expecting to receive an urn containing my mother's earthly remains!" The scenario was not in the least amusing but the fact that the police had taken it upon themselves to deliver this in person still tempted Luc Mathieu to smile.

"Perhaps you had better open the parcel Mr Mathieu!" Obviously the officer of the law now considered he had toyed with the introductions for long enough.

Possibly because he was faced with the inevitable Luc took the parcel and commenced opening it. This, he deemed was not the correct manner by which one should treat such an article, but apparently it was something he was now expected to do. Still with the parcel finally opened Luc did not see what he had expected to find inside.

"What is this, is it some sort of joke?" The young man looked at the contents with something that approached disgust for inside there was no urn containing his parent's remains but a box containing what appeared to his eyes to be a load of junk.

"These are drugs Mr Mathieu! Can you tell me how these came into your possession?" The Inspector's must have raised his voice a few notches on the word drugs for ears that were craning to listen from the outside of that room suddenly started upright as if they were hearing things and then almost immediately gathered together in order to air their views on what this young pretender was now involved in.

"But these have never been in my possession neither was I expecting them. Surely there must be some mistake?" Once again Luc's eyes focussed on the girl for after all it appeared that she was supposed to be the courier but then the girl looked so young and innocent.

"Yet the parcel was addressed to you at this address, and for your information Mr Mathieu these also happen to be class A drugs which are considered to be illegal in this country. Tell me did you seek to have these delivered for your own consumption or are you one of that unfortunate breed that seek to spread misery on our streets!"

"I do not take drugs. I have never taken drugs and what is more the parcel that I was expecting contained the ashes of my departed mother!" Luc clenched his knuckles. Really he could well do without all this.

"And why would you be expecting your mother's ashes to be delivered by courier Mr Mathieu?"

"My mother died in France where she had lived for many years after being declared a social outcast because she chose to marry someone who was not of this country. I required her ashes to be sent here so that I could at least see the woman had a decent burial alongside of her ancestors!"

"If that was the case then why did you not bring the ashes with you on your own return? I believe you have recently been in France!"

"I attended the funeral but as I was summoned here for the reading of the will appertaining to the family estate, I had to leave orders at the crematorium to forward the same after they had duly attended to matters!"

"You have lived in France all of your life, you have a French name, therefore for what reason did you seek to travel to England with or without your mother's remains?"

"Because it so happens that as the only living descendant of my grandfather, I had inherited the Priory Manor and the lands around it. In actual fact the solicitor in charge of the last will and testament of Edward Bardon insisted that it was my duty to be here on site!"

"So you employed a courier firm to deliver your mother's ashes to you?"

"Yes, tell me did I do wrong?"

"Miss Taylor here claims that she was the one who supposedly worked for this firm!" So now the girl had been included in the conversation. Luc glanced across at her to be met with impassive silence for at the time Jayne was still wondering how on earth she was going to explain this delay to her employers for surely it must now appear that the employ she had recently taken would be terminated forthwith. Plus the fact that there was still her brother's bike out there somewhere and she doubted whether Robert would ever forgive her for losing this most precious of his objects.

"Then Miss Taylor must be the one who was charged to take receipt of the parcel from one of the crew from a cross channel ferry boat!" Now it sounded worse as far as she was concerned. The crewman had empathically denied passing her any such parcel, this of course was what had led to her own involvement in the case yet as no crewman admitted responsibility for handing this to her then it must appear that her own story was even more suspect as to where she had received the drugs from.

"The matter requires further investigation. In the meantime I feel that I must caution the two of you. In the intervening period whilst I complete such investigations I shall require the pair of you to remain in the vicinity and I would therefore be obliged if you handed your passports over to my second in command. As you yourself are of French nationality Mr Mathieu it will be necessary for me to contact my opposing number in France. You look disturbed Miss Taylor?"

"I'm afraid that I do not have my passport with me for I did not deem it necessary to make a journey on English soil!"

"That is no hardship Miss Taylor. If you furnish us with your home address one of my colleagues will collect it for you for you yourself will be required to abide within the strict boundaries of this county. Any deviation will lead to your immediate arrest. Once I have resolved the matter with my colleagues however I will be in touch with you both. And now Mr Mathieu I believe that you yourself are presently entertaining we therefore need detain you no longer at the moment. But please be aware that this is a very serious matter therefore you would be well advised to abide by our instructions!"

"But what am I supposed to do now?" For a moment Luc was convinced that the girl's eyes flashed.

"You will abide by the rules we have just set out Miss Taylor. Any deviation from these will result in your immediate arrest and therefore I believe you would much prefer to spend the intervening period in the outside world rather than in a penitentiary!"

The Inspector had obviously exhausted what he had to say and thus he motioned to his fellow officer that they were about to leave not forgetting the parcel that they had brought with them. For her part Jayne looked completely aghast for now she had little idea as to what she was supposed to do. Her bike was still missing, she was far away from home and furthermore she was now compelled to remain in an area that she knew little about. It was Luc who noticed her expression.

"I take it that you are stranded here Miss Taylor?"

"Something like that! Mr Mathieu I would like to say that I had nothing to do with any switch in those parcels and despite what the Inspector says I did take delivery of it from one of the seamen from off the ferry boat as was previously arranged!"

"Maybe I do not know why but I feel inclined to believe you Miss Taylor. But as you are now obviously stranded the least that I can do is to offer you my hospitality at Priory Manor. It is a large house and therefore we have plenty of unused space. Therefore with your permission I will ask my housekeeper to make up a room here for you!"

Jayne swallowed hard. In truth folk are often known to come out with the absurd at such moments and Jayne was no exception to this rule for almost without thinking what she was saying she allowed the words to leave her lips. "But what about my bike? My brother will kill me if anything happens to it!"

For a moment a fleeting smile passed across Luc's face. "Once you are settled and I have dealt with the group of people still waiting for my presence, we will easily deal with that matter. In the meantime I will leave you in the very capable hands of my housekeeper!" He rang a bell and a middle aged woman appeared

For her part Mrs Bentham appeared none too pleased at her master's request to prepare yet another bedroom. Yet as far as she was concerned he was still the master of the Hall and consequently she was required to do his bidding even if the person he was doing this for appeared to have no luggage and was dressed in those ridiculous leathers that male motor cyclists appeared to rage about. Consequently she nodded with an apparent bad grace and once again Jayne was to find herself left alone in that room with only her thoughts for company.

Chapter Two

Looking around at the place Jayne presumed that during the summer the windows of that room would give an excellent view of the garden along with all of its foliage, but at this time of the year the only image she received was one of a stark absence of life for no green shoots had yet appeared on the bushes which had suffered the ravages of the winter chills. She had heard that august party leave and was quite convinced that more than one of them took a peek inside the room where she currently was possibly wondering in their own minds who exactly this creature was and why she had come here to sully the atmosphere of the place. Of course they might well be excused for such thoughts for after all they were in fact still reeling after the contents of that will had been made public and more than one person resented the fact that Luc Mathieu, the son of the one who had left the Hall in disgrace, should have inherited almost everything apart from a few tokens which had been passed on to several menial workers.

One of the things that roused their anger the most was the fact that this man's mother who had left in disgrace many years previously had a brother who by rights should have been the one to have inherited, only unfortunately that individual had chosen to die before his maturity and thus they considered that life was not very fair.

For her part Jayne was still standing in her leathers when Luc finally entered the room. She was still wearing these things because quite frankly she had no other clothes which she could have changed into, at least none with her. After all Jayne Taylor had never dreamed when she had left home that she would be so delayed and thus by this time, not having had the clinging leather outfit off her body since leaving home, they were beginning to irritate her more than a little.

Still Luc for one apparently did not notice her dress for it appeared that he had one thing only on his mind and that was to try and obtain the truth from this girl. To his mind if she had been caught peddling drugs then what had she done with the parcel he was expecting to receive, the one that he had gone out of his way in arranging for his mother's remains to be transported by ferry and had employed this courier firm to collect the same from off the ferryboat. Thus quite naturally his first inclination was that this girl had somehow, for reasons of her own, substituted the drugs for the parcel that she should have been carrying.

One supposes that viewed in the light of day many flaws could have been found in his reasoning but by this time Luc Mathieu had ceased to be interested in any alternative version of events.

"As we now appear to have the house to ourselves perhaps you will now tell me why on earth you decided to substitute parcels before you left the port Miss Taylor?"

"I substituted nothing!" Her hackles rising Jayne confronted him now with a red face little realising that the top button of her jacket had now managed to free itself loosening the zip which lay below, all of which served to make her look more attractive. "The parcel that I received from the seaman happens to be the same one that the police were able to present you with this morning!"

"Then how did this seaman managed to get drugs ashore if that is what you are inferring?"

"I am afraid that is something that I do not know. Perhaps you could find the answer to that conundrum if you went and asked him!"

"I don't think that will be necessary because somehow I am beginning to believe your far- fetched story. Indeed there must be some truth in it because I am also beginning to believe that the alternative is just too silly to contemplate!"

"Then I have no doubt that you have already formed your own views on the matter!" Her voice was cutting, she did not want to be patronised. In fact she did not know what she was supposed to be doing in this house, but there again she supposed that she had been offered little alternative.

"Not exactly! But tell me is that rubber thing the only object you have to wear?" Now she supposed he was being critical about her appearance---what else did he expect a courier to be wearing?

"When I left home in order to complete a job of work I never imagined that this would entail a stay in some country manor. If I had any previous notion that this was likely to happen then I would have packed a suitcase!"

"So you are saying that you have nothing else to wear other than your leathers?" At least she supposed he had decided to call her gear by the correct name. Perhaps she ought to be thankful for that!

"Obviously I have nothing else to wear and as a matter of fact these are not even my leathers for they belong to my brother!"

"Then won't he be missing them?"

"Not at the moment, you see he has no need of them in Afghanistan, nor has he any need of his bike at the moment either, at least not until he is able to come home on leave!"

"In that case I will run you into Canterbury so that you can get yourself fixed up!" He had already produced his car keys as if this would be a forgone conclusion and she would agree with profound thanks.

"Not having any cash on me I am afraid that I must decline your offer!" She had no need of cash when she was supposed to be simply doing a job plus the fact until she was paid by the courier service she had little of it to spare,

"In that case Miss Taylor you may charge it to my account for I have no wish to see you wandering around the Hall for goodness knows how long clad only in that riding gear!" So he was a man who made quick decisions for even now he had moved to stand by the door expecting her to follow. "No doubt Mrs Bentham will have finished off your room for you when we return even if she is in a mood at the moment not to be hurried!"

So here she was in the midst of the shopping centre in Canterbury dropped off by a man who had informed her before he left that he would return to pick her up in an hour's time at the place where he had dropped her off. Her hand moved to her pocket to touch the wallet which he had stuffed full of notes before thrusting it at her before he left stating he considered that would be sufficient enough to get something that would make her look a little more presentable and quite frankly there was enough money in that wallet to fulfil all her needs. She idly wondered what he would have done if she had made for the station with the money instead in an effort to get home but then reminded herself that this also was not possible because of the police curfew on her movements.

Consequently the only thing left for her to do was to make for the shops in order to equip herself. After all she could always repay the man at some later stage, although with the amount he had given to her it was likely to be at a much later stage. Still perhaps the surprise was his when she returned to the meeting place at the appropriate time her leathers now neatly packed away in a box and wearing some of the articles she had purchased.

"I would say that it is a most pleasant surprise to see you actually looking more like a woman!" He took in her well defined features, her skin texture that could hardly be confused with that of a male and that blonde hair which now flowed more easily over the dress she was wearing and perhaps he realised for the first time that she was one attractive female as she made to enter the car.

"No doubt Mrs Bentham will now have a meal waiting for us! One can hardly call it lunch at this time of the day I suppose but no doubt it will serve to suffice at any time" It was the only thing he could think of to say as he started up the car and he hoped with all of his heart that the housekeeper had seen fit to do this. Then remembering the parcel she had placed in the back of the vehicle. "That I presume is your brother's riding gear?"

"Along with a little underwear and nightwear that I will obviously need: Although there is still one thing I have not yet re-cooped for him and that is the bike!"

Luc sighed as he cast a look in her direction. "You never give up do you Miss Taylor. But if it will alleviate your worries we do have plenty of room to store the bike at the Manor therefore I will take you to the police compound myself in the pick-up for you to collect it once I have satisfied myself with your story. For you see I am still anxious to know where the urn containing my mother's ashes has disappeared to!"

Perhaps Jayne had expected Luc to demand answers there and then but the man was obviously in no hurry not that was until they had eaten and Mrs Bentham had cleared the room sniffing in her indomitable way that indicated she considered things were not right for why should this chit of a girl who had come to the Hall with a police escort now presume she could be waited on like the landed gentry?

"I think that she has probably got it in for you therefore you will have to watch your back!" Luc himself laughed at the woman's expression before turning to talk of more serious matters.

"According to your story you were hired by the courier firm to collect this parcel from off one of the seamen from the ferry boat and then deliver the parcel here?"

"That is correct!" She wondered how many more times she would be required to repeat this story.

"If it helps at all I myself gave such orders to my contact in France and according to what he has just E-mailed me, then for his part that was exactly what he did. Therefore the urn actually left Calais in a parcel addressed to me!"

"In that case what happened to it?"

"That is a very good question Miss Taylor and one that I am determined to find the answer to I was unable to wait in order to bring the urn home myself, you may remember the group of folk braying for my blood when you first arrived. But I had been summoned by the solicitor and they are not people one goes out of ones way to offend. On the other hand it seems to be rather far-fetched to suggest that someone deliberately chose my parcel to substitute their own goods in, would you not agree?"

"By that I presume that you like the police are blaming me for such a transfer?"

"Actually dear girl I am not. If you had drugs to disperse I think it hardly likely that you would have been there to meet a ferry to collect them from a seaman who now presumably does not exist! By the way I have decided that Miss Taylor seems to be a little formal considering you will probably be spending some time here. Well you do have nowhere else to go in this part of the country and this is the part you are confined to. Anyway perhaps you will not mind if I therefore call you Jayne?"

"Mr Mathieu -----!" She began but was quickly silenced.

"What is good for the goose is also good for the gander therefore the name is Luc if you don't mind!"

She glanced across at him and decided that Luc Mathieu had a very nice smile when he decided to exercise his face. But then the man had obviously not finished with her.

"There must be some people who are currently wondering where you are at this moment in time; your parents for instance. Have you managed to contact them yet?"

"I'm afraid that I left my mobile in my pannier!" The confession sounded weak she had to admit and in truth she felt a little ashamed of not thinking of them before although if she was honest she would have admitted that having to confess her predicament to her mother was something that she positively abhorred.

"Well there happens to be a telephone here so perhaps you had better contact them. It might possibly be better if you said that you were staying with friends so as not to worry them unduly!"

For a moment she wondered whether he had read the reluctance in her thoughts but nevertheless Jayne went to the phone dutifully like a small child who had been rebuked. Of course her mother was chatty and wanted to know where she was and when she was coming back for in truth they had expected to have seen the girl back that morning. Consequently she found that Luc's suggestion that she was staying with friends came in very useful. She had also thought of ringing the courier firm but as assignments were taken rather freelance she felt she could hardly admit to what had happened, let alone having her bike impounded whilst she herself had been confined within certain territorial limits. For if she had done this then surely this would have meant having to forego any such jobs in the future and in the future was the time when she would probably need them.

He was waiting for her as she finished her rhetoric and they left Mrs Bentham to clear away without waiting around to hear her criticism. After that it was a peaceful drive in the pick-up truck back to the coast, something which she could not help but contrast with her last journey along these roads in the police car when she had been nervous and on edge.

Luc also was right when he had said he could foresee no difficulty in them collecting the bike from the compound and if any of the police thereabouts attempted to recognise her then now dressed more like a female she easily out witted them. They were in fact about to make back again to the Hall when Jayne spotted a certain individual she was sure that she recognised and a quick intake of breath made Luc look at her as she realised that this was the missing seaman the one who had handed her the parcel.

"What's the matter now?" His question was legitimate enough.

"The man, the one we passed back there, I am sure that was the seaman who gave me the parcel: The seaman who is not supposed to exist!"

She heard the sharp intake of breath as Luc stopped the truck eager now to be able to support her story but then by this time the sighting had well and truly disappeared. "Are you sure that was same the fellow you spotted?" Perhaps his own disappointment almost sounded as if he now doubted her words.

Jayne nodded. The fact that the man had now disappeared came as a disappointment to her and she prayed that the one by her side actually believed her story. Yet it was Luc who left the vehicle now anxious to ascertain whether he could see anything of this illusive character for himself and failing in his quest his face darkened.

"I guess that was pretty futile, perhaps we had better head back to Priory Manor!" There was something in his expression when he climbed back into the truck which made her decide to change the subject.

"Your mother, she must have died young, had she been ill?" The words sounded trite she knew but her efforts at changing the subject appeared to have paid off.

"She had breast cancer which refused to react to any form of treatment and perhaps after her miserable existence she was not sorry to go. I'm sorry, but of course you are not acquainted with the full story. When she married my father against her parent's wishes she was practically drummed out of the family. In a way they were probably right in voicing their objections to my father for after landing her with a child he then took it into his head to disappear and was not seen after that. Consequently my mother, a foreigner in France and unable to return to her own folk was forced to scrimp and save in order to bring me up. Not only did she take a full time job to pay her way in the world but she also took in washing to provide the means for my education. Yet even whilst she was dying I was unable to stay by her side because of events that transpired in England and as ill as she was my mother insisted that I should pay my respects to her father. It was at his funeral that I received news of my own mother's demise yet even at that point I was not allowed to spend any time after her funeral in France for I was suddenly summoned back to England for the reading of my grandfather's will. In doing so I had to depend on the funeral undertakers to forward my mother's ashes so that at least I could finally take her home. The rest I believe you are already acquainted with, the parcel I was expecting did not contain my mother's remains and no doubt you will have guessed from the gathering when you arrived at the Hall that I was not the favoured one to be a beneficiary at that reading!"

"That is a sad story!" She could not help but exude her sympathy and remembering the dour faces of those who had left just after her own arrival at the place seemed to make the situation even worse. "But then surely if your mother's ashes were dispatched from France by the undertakers then they must be somewhere, perhaps even close at hand!" Her words were intended to convey this sympathy she now felt for the man but Luc glanced at her almost as if he was still a little unsure of her motives.

"That is why when you said you thought you had spotted the seaman who passed the packet on to you I was anxious to question him myself even if he initially said that he was never on that boat. But in our quest we appeared to be as ill-fated as my relatives felt when they realised that the Hall had been passed on to me!"

"Your mother had a brother I believe you said?" Why she persisted in carrying on with this conversation Jayne did not know. It just seemed to do Luc good to be able to unburden his soul to a comparative stranger.

"She had and he was present when my mother was evicted from her home and never spoke in her defence. But then life seems to have a peculiar way of repeating itself. John was a soldier and unfortunately he was killed in one of the skirmishes that this country seems to go out of its way to find. Yet although my mother was now left next of kin her father never deemed to contact her or attempt to close the rift that her marriage had brought to the family. Therefore as much as she would have liked to at the time my mother never came home. That is why I am now determined that her ashes will be taken and laid to rest in their rightful place!"

"Thank you for telling me all of this!" Jayne felt a little humbled at this confidence but in return he then turned to her.

"Now you have heard my story perhaps you will now tell me your own. I am actually fascinated as to why a mere chit of a girl should want to undertake a man's job for starters?"

"The answer to that is quite simple. I took on the role simply because it was a job and they are rather hard to come by in the present climate. I had no fear of riding for I had been out with Robert many times and therefore it seemed only natural for me to make use of his bike and his other gear in his absence!"

"I guess you are a girl full of surprises!" She glanced at him thinking at first he was perhaps being sarcastic, but there was nothing like that muted in his expression for it was one of pure interest.

Still there was not a great deal left to say before they arrived back at the Hall and finding that Mrs Bentham had now decided to complete her room, Jayne made her excuses. Luc Mathieu certainly had no need of being pestered by her with all he currently had to think about for himself.

Jayne was still familiarising herself with the Hall and diligently removing dust covers from the places that she deemed were spoiled by their presence, in spite of Mrs Bentham's disapproving looks, when the first of two visitors arrived to disturb the calm both Luc and Jayne had begun to experience by being left alone.

Still it can be said that the sight of the police car outside in the drive did much to upset this state of equilibrium for perhaps both of them had begun to push the thought of the police to the back of their minds. Neither could it be said that the Detective Inspector wished to conduct his business on the doorstep for the man rapidly pushed past them inviting himself into the house and waited for Luc to show him into a room where he could conduct his business.

"The girl I wish her also to hear what I have to say!" The policeman blustered acting very much as if he believed that Luc had secretly spirited her away.

"In that case I will go and get her!" Luc made but a simple call in the doorway before they were joined by the one the policeman had specified. Mind you the officer did look at Jayne twice when she entered the room as if deciding whether this was the right girl now that she had discarded her leathers.

"First of all as far as you are concerned Mr Mathieu I can now confirm that a certain firm of undertakers resident in France and who were responsible for the disposal of your mother's remains, did in effect place the urn of her ashes in a parcel addressed to yourself on a certain ferry boat that was crossing the channel and that such a parcel was expected to be retrieved from the docks in England by a courier firm to transport the same to the Hall here. Yet although that part of the story happens to be true it still does not explain how you yourself Miss Taylor came to be in receipt of a parcel of drugs which if they had been on that ferry had escaped all forms of detection and apparently were not handed to you by a member of the crew. Have you anything that you can add to this Miss Taylor?"

Jayne looked flummoxed and it was Luc who now came to her rescue. "Nothing at all apart from the fact that Jayne believed she spotted the seaman who passed her the parcel at the docks when we returned there in order to collect the bike!"

"And you obtained this person's identity by some means?"

"Unfortunately the man disappeared before we were able to do any such thing!"

Perhaps Jayne now expected the policeman to pooh-pooh any such sighting but instead the man still appeared to be interested. "According to our French counterparts a certain quantity of drugs appeared to have been removed from their country at a time which could well have coincided with the sailing of that ferry. Even so no traces of drugs were apparently found on the vessel!" In retrospect Jayne believed the policeman was thinking aloud rather than speaking to her but Luc certainly took him up on his warbling.

"Never mind talking about the drugs, what about my mother's ashes? I know for a fact that they were delivered to the docks by the undertaker for transportation, therefore have they been found on board?"

"Not at the moment Mr Mathieu although I understand your concern and we will make every effort to seek them out. In the meantime I think that perhaps you can consider yourself free from our investigations!"

"If that is a fact then what about Miss Taylor?"

"Miss Taylor remains an integral part of our investigations I am afraid and therefore she must consider herself to be still confined to the area; and of course we will require an address where she can be contacted and where she can regularly report to the local police from!"

"Miss Taylor already has an address, it happens to be here!" The Inspector looked surprised at Luc's response; perhaps he had thought that with Luc being removed from their investigations then the girl would have left the Hall. Nevertheless having completed his appointed task the man shrugged his shoulders before taking his leave.

"Thank you for that!" Jayne glanced up in Luc's direction.

"And what else was I supposed to do? Where on earth where you supposed to go around here without money to support you?"

He had moved away from her at the time and Jayne had been left feeling a little dispirited. After all she had thought that she and Luc were beginning to get on but then of course she had forgotten that Luc was of course now the owner of Priory Manor and she was simply a mere acquaintance.

Still if Luc had any aspirations of grandeur, all such thought were removed with the advent of their next visitor. Bumbling and fretting that all this work was far too much in regard to one will it was the solicitor who was the one to grace the doorstep of the Hall and who was dutifully shown into the room that the Inspector had just vacated.

"Mr Mathieu I am afraid that I have to inform you that the will which I read out in this building quite recently, has now been contested! I must say before I continue that this comes as a great inconvenience to me!"

"It is an inconvenience not only to you Sir!" Jayne saw Luc's lips tighten. She supposed it was not really her place to be in the same room as the pair at this time but no words had been said to this effect and Luc for his part, seemed to welcome her presence.

"No matter for it is imperative that we should clear up this business as soon as possible!"

"Then perhaps you will be good enough Sir to inform me what I am supposed to do about the matter? Perhaps you would be good enough to explain on what grounds the will has been contested and as a matter of interest by whom?"

"The will has been contested by your second cousin who goes under the name of Stuart Bardon. In the first place it has been suggested that after your uncle was killed Edward Bardon made out a second will thus making the original one null and void. I must add however that up until this moment no such will has been produced. It has also been suggested that you are not the legitimate son of Ellen Bardon !"

"But I have already produced my birth certificate to prove my identity!"

"Not necessarily enough Mr Mathieu for it is always possible that you were adopted at birth for reasons known only to Ellen Bardon!"

"And if I say that I take offence at your suggestion Mr Withers?"

"I am afraid that cannot be accepted as the proof of your birth Mr Mathieu. It appears that your relatives were surprised that Ellen ever gave birth as she had long been considered to be infertile in family circles. I can only suggest that if you wish to prove these assumptions made by the family to be incorrect then a D.N.A. test might be considered to be helpful."

"Then I take it that you doubt my word?"

"Not necessarily Mr Mathieu. But as the family obtained such a sample from Edward Bardon before he was buried it might be to your advantage to be able to prove their assumptions wrong!"

Jayne noticed how Luc's face had now flushed up and anxious to prevent a scene which in the present circumstances would do no good at all, she laid her hand on his shoulder. "Then such a test is easy to obtain?" Now it was the solicitors turn to glare in her direction as if he was wondering who this chit of a girl was who had dared to enter into what he considered to be a private conversation. Still his client looked at him as if he supported what the girl had said.

"Of course, I am sure that your doctor will be able to arrange such a test to be undertaken locally at the hospital!"

"Then I am sure that Mr Mathieu will abide by such rules!" It was Jayne again who then appeared to interject much to the solicitor's consternation. Who on earth was this girl and what had such business got to do with her?

Her companion however seemed to accept her words and the solicitor was left shaking his head in some disbelief.

"In that case I will leave the matter in your hands Mr Mathieu and you will supply me with the results of such a test when they are forthcoming. No you need not bother I will show myself out for after all I am quite familiar with the layout of this place!" Perceiving that he was unlikely to gain anymore on the subject matter the solicitor made to leave in what can be described as ill grace.

"I'm sorry; I guess I shouldn't have interfered into matters that were after all none of my business!" Upon the solicitor's departure, the man of letters obviously believing he had achieved something if the expression on his face was anything to go by, Jayne realising that perhaps she had interjected when it was not required made haste to apologise for her behaviour. In truth she had objected to seeing Luc standing there apparently at a loss for words when the accusation had been put to him.

"I admit that I am rather glad that you did!" The man smiled whimsically at her in return. "I guess what the man had to say left me feeling a little speechless!"

"Then under the circumstances it is perhaps better if you do what the man suggested even if you do disagree with his argument!"

"I have not yet got a doctor in this country though!" She determined that Luc was still at a loss after what had happened.

"Well getting one is not all that difficult. I'm sure if you go to your nearest Primary Health Care then some practitioner will be only too pleased to include you on his list. After all it should not be too difficult for them to obtain your previous medical records from France!"

"Everything seems to be going wrong at the moment. First of all there is the disappearance of my mother's ashes and now this-------!" He broke off suddenly perhaps realising that he had pushed other matters into the background. "Still it is not me that we should be worrying about for at least I appear to have been cleared by the police. On the other hand you still appear to be on their list of suspects, all of which leaves me to say that we should be doing something about finding that man you saw back in Dover and not bothering about doctors or medical records. After all I do not need anyone to prove who I am; my mother's word was quite good enough for me!"

"There is no reason why we should not be able to do both. First we must sort out a doctor for you and once your tests are underway then we can look again for this man. Make no mistake Luc I am as anxious to find him and clear my name as what you are in order to retrieve your mother's ashes but it is just a question of priorities!"

"Has anyone told you what a remarkable girl you are Jayne Taylor?"

"Maybe my luck changed when I met you" Jayne who had returned to the task of pumping up cushions paused and looked at him in return.

"That is all the more reason why we need to find this seaman or whoever he is. If indeed he is a seaman and your account of him seems to indicate that he is, then the chances are we will stand a better opportunity of catching up with him around that port. Tell me though, why do you feel you have to pump up the cushions like that for surely that is Mrs Bentham's job?"

"Perhaps it is because I like to see the place looking as if it is lived in and not just covered up with dust sheets and at least the cushions do bring a little welcome colour to the place against that Victorian brown!" She stopped suddenly realising that it was after all not her place to criticise the furnishings of his dwelling. She was merely a guest here and without Luc's kind auspices she would have had nowhere to go.

"Someday I am sure you will make someone an excellent wife. Tell me Jayne is there such a man in your life?"

Jayne thought about Simon with his pompous attitude and shivered as she shook her head. The man it was true considered himself to be her fiancé but that was not the way that Jayne understood matters and therefore she could be forgiven for this slight untruth "No there is not and according to my mother I am still far too young to even contemplate such matters!" Well she supposed that part was at least true!

"Why how old are you exactly then because if you are still a juvenile no doubt the police should have taken that factor into consideration before they arrested you?"

"At twenty two one can hardly be considered to be a juvenile especially when one has a degree to one's name!" She had not really wanted to admit this for she realised what his next question would be and sure enough he was not slow in providing it.

"Then if you are blessed with such qualifications would it be rude to enquire exactly why you sought work as a courier?"

"Maybe you have not heard about the recession in France for the job I earned when I entered the labour market managed to fold and the firm went into liquidation. Therefore at times such as this it is not so surprising when one is willing to take any job to keep the so-called wolf from the door. But what about you, I know little enough about your past apart from the fact that you were brought up in France and inherited this property through the demise of others?"

"Maybe we should go and see if any practitioner will accept me on their list!" Somehow Luc appeared reluctant to speak about the past, but then she supposed that was not really surprising with having the death of his mother on his hands.

"Of course, please forgive my curiosity!" She moved in the direction of the door and Luc caught her by the arm.

"I am sorry; it was uncharitable of me not to respond to your question. But after we have finished all our chores then perhaps I will tell you all about France!"

"I think perhaps the reverse can be said to be order for what would I have done if our paths had never crossed? Would I currently be gracing some police cell?

It proved remarkably simple for Luc to place himself on a doctor's list at the Centre; more especially when he was able to give his address as Priory Manor and upon mention of that name Jayne witnessed several of the younger members of staff at the place beginning to regard Luc in a new light. The appointment for the D.N.A testing however was something upon which he was forced to wait, at least until the establishment had obtained his previous medical records from his former doctor in France.

Still the proposed waiting period for this did not appear to unduly worry Luc for now he had it in mind to return to that port in search of the mysterious seaman whom Jayne had sworn to have seen again since the incident, but whom she now felt that she had little hope of making any contact with him again.

"Well we can but try, nothing ventured, nothing gained or so they say!" Perhaps in a way he was trying to be cheerful, or maybe he wanted simply to forget his own forthcoming appointment with the hospital. Thinking back to his own French connection Jayne found that she had a wealth of questions to ask him by the time they were back in the car and heading towards the coast.

"Your English is perfect Luc. How come you don't have any trace of an accent?"

He glanced at her a little puzzled before he made his response. "Maybe that was because I was brought up to speak English at home for once my father had left the nest my mother was determined that I should loose nothing of what she considered to be my native tongue!"

"So you have never seen your father since he left home?"

"No, neither have I any desire to meet him, not after what he did to my mother. Of course I had to speak a certain amount of French both at school and when I went on for further studies, but English still remained my first language for my mother never forgot her home even if she had initially been drummed out of it. Perhaps that is why I am so eager to bring back her remains so that she can at last rest in peace!"

"That is a sad story Luc!"

"Maybe, but now our prime intention is to see if we can see any signs of that man, the seaman you spoke about!"

"But I don't expect that he will be wearing his crew member's uniform by this time!"

"Such ratings are often peculiar fellows. Anyway you did manage to get a good look at his features!"

Jayne wished she was as confident as what Luc was that she would spot this person but then there were a great many people around that area and to be able to spot one man with surety was almost like looking for a needle in a haystack.

Still perhaps fortune often makes one jolt in surprise for it had to be on the promenade when she spotted that figure yet again and from his condition he looked almost as if he had just left one watering hole and was heading for another.

Luc stopped the car as she gasped out in surprise. "Don't be so surprised for sometimes these folk are creatures of habit. Well are we going to get out of this contraption and find out for certain?"

He had stopped the car on the promenade almost adjacent to where the man was walking and therefore Jayne had little difficulty in confronting the sailor, the only trouble was she suddenly found that her mouth had dried up and she didn't know what to say. Fortunately it was again Luc who came to her rescue but then she reminded herself he also had a vested interest in this person

"I believe you handed Miss Taylor a parcel the other evening, a task you were charged to do by someone on the ferry boat?"

The man shook his head obviously feeling a little perplexed. "You seem to have the wrong person if you are speaking to me governor!"

"Perhaps you do not recognise Miss Taylor at the moment for at that time she was working as a courier and was dressed in leathers?"

The seaman shifted uneasily and looked over his shoulder. "I did as I was charged to do, what's wrong in that?"

"I could ask you how you managed to get through security carrying that parcel?"

"That is probably because I never went through any security for I never worked on that boat!"

"In that case how did you manage to get hold of the package?"

"That was easy it was brought in on a fishing vessel. How it got there I do not know and I do not go around asking questions. I was simply paid for my efforts and I guess I am not shy in being able to earn an odd quid or so when I am on shore leave!"

"You were on shore leave at the time and that is why you were wearing your ratings uniform?"

"Of course because it stands one in good stead if you happen to be partaking in some free- lance work around the port!"

"And what about the people who were on the fishing vessel?"

"Here, what is this all about: I did a bloke a favour and the courier or girl as it turns out to be got the parcel she had been waiting for, so what was the harm in that?"

"Maybe the police will be able to answer that question for you!"

"Here I want none of that. That lot are always sticking their noses into someone else's business and when they do there are no prizes for guessing who comes worst off. Therefore as far as those flat foots are concerned I shall deny everything. And now I will say good day to you!" The seaman was obviously ready to make his escape.

"Before you go you could at least tell us what fishing boat you were speaking about?"

"And why should I want to do that. I'm not after putting my mates in trouble?"

"Tell me have you any idea what this parcel should have contained?"

"I guess that had nothing to do with me!"

"As a matter of fact I was the one waiting for the parcel to be delivered to me. By rights it should have contained my mother's ashes. The fact that it didn't is enough to make me feel concerned!"

The seaman who had been about to make his way away from them suddenly paused. It was almost that the thought of an urn of ashes being lost had now put a different complexion on matters.

"I can only tell you what I heard. As I wasn't there myself at the time I cannot say that it is the truth but from what I heard the parcel was thrown from the ferry boat into the fishing vessel on its journey across the channel and why anyone would want to do that with a casket of ashes is quite beyond me."

Chapter Three

"But surely we ought to report this?" Jayne expressed her incredulity as Luc shook his head, for to her it made common sense that they should report this sighting and what was more they should report the matter without delay.

"I don't think so, at least not at this moment in time for even if the police took our account seriously which I very much doubt, I cannot think that our tract with this man would be allowed to continue. So far we have only got part of the story from him and I am sure that there is still a lot more that he could tell us. Who, for example is the owner of this fishing boat and why did they deem it necessary to offload their advantage? To me it sounds ridiculous that the folk on the ferry boat should want to find an ally with a fishing vessel!" Luc's words sounded so definite that much as she would have liked to, Jayne did not think to argue for in all truth it was Luc's mother's ashes that had apparently gone missing and therefore it was fitting that perhaps he should have the final say on the matter, although in all truth Jayne still believed that the police ought to know about the man they had seen and indeed spoken to.

Perhaps this decision was something which later she came to regret for it was only a couple of days later when picking up the local newspaper there was an account of a certain person's mysterious death and from the description that the paper gave of him it also sounded very much like the naval rating that they had met close to the port, the one who had spoken about fishing boat and a specific cargo being unloaded.

"Have you seen this?" Her hands still shaking Jayne hastily sought Luc out, much perhaps to the other person's annoyance as he was at the time in the midst of a shave in preparation for a visit to the hospital for the sample for D.N.A. testing to be carried out.

"I have hardly had the time to see anything in the present circumstances. What is it anyway?"

"The man whom we were speaking to close to the port the other day; the naval rating who apparently found the need to utilise his time away from his more formal duties so that he could frequent fishing boats!"

"So what about him?" Despite the manner of his response which was short and clipped Luc had obviously felt an interest for he paused now with his shaver still in his hand.

"He has been found dead and the authorities are not ruling out foul play!"

Upon her words Luc finally decided to put down his shaver and take the paper off her. "But how do you know that we are talking about the same person? For after all the whole area is usually swarming with naval ratings before or after their contract has started or expired. It is after all a seaport. Besides there is no picture of this man here that enables one to identify him so why so you suppose it is our man?"

"Call it feminine intuition if you like. I still think we should have gone to the police with our findings!"

"And no doubt by this time we would both have been on the suspect list. Oh all right I can see that there is no other way to satisfy your curiosity on this issue therefore once I have been to the hospital about the other matter we will go there. At least that ought to prevent you from sulking in my direction for the rest of the day!"

Jayne grimaced in the face of the one who had uttered these words but nevertheless said nothing. After all it was quite possible that Luc was right after all and that this poor person had nothing at all to do with the man that they had met. Still Luc proved to be as good as his word. The hospital visit didn't take long even if Jayne's presence with Luc did appear to be questioned for it was considered that after all one seldom needed a companion for a simple blood test and therefore Luc was looked at as something of a freak as he apparently desired female company for this.

"Oh this is my cousin!" Luc, sensing the mood, made haste to explain her presence. "She has recently been bereaved and therefore I am looking after her! Therefore I still feel it a little unwise to leave her on her own!" Jayne scowled at the words which demeaned her as someone possibly suffering from a traumatic event, even if this rhetoric did appear to be enough to satisfy the hospital authorities as they nodded and then glanced in her direction sympathetically.

Therefore the two of them were soon heading towards the port and more in particular the police station which was located there with Jayne still grumbling as to why Luc had described her as being his bereaved cousin.

In all probability the desk sergeant was more than a little surprised to see them for he certainly didn't consider that this was the time destined for Jayne Taylor to check in as she had been so ordered. Moreover the two of them appeared to be brandishing a newspaper in their hands and seemingly expecting him to both see and read the contents whilst the paper still floated above his head whilst at the time the officer had been more concerned with his telephone.

"The man who was killed, the naval rating, it is possible that we met him just a couple of days ago. Perhaps this is important and we should tell the Inspector about this meeting!"

"I am afraid that the Inspector is not available at the moment!" The young desk sergeant clutched the desk top as he spoke knowing that it would be more than his job was worth to have said differently, a factor which looking at his face made Jayne decide that the man was not exactly telling the truth. "Under the circumstances therefore perhaps you could relate your business to me and I have no doubt that the Inspector will contact you later if he believes this to be of some importance!" The man had stated both his case and the solution to the problem as he saw it and now he apparently resembled some plumped up chicken if the expression on his face was anything to go by.

"Perhaps we should wait for I am sure that the Inspector will believe our message to be of some importance!" Jayne almost took a delight in watching the other's face change at hearing this and believing that his peace was about to be shattered. But there again the desk sergeant vaguely remembered the girl from a past encounter even if this time around she was wearing female clothing and he also knew that she had a habit of getting what she wanted. In all truth he did not know what to do about the situation for he knew full well that the Inspector was currently in his room and had given orders that he was not to be disturbed and what was more people disobeyed such an order at their peril.

"If that is what you want to do then you can wait but he may be some time!" The desk sergeant suddenly felt defeated with their argument. Nevertheless he left them waiting a good fifteen minutes hoping that they would tire of the situation and leave before he himself began to tire of their presence in the office as he was beginning to feel he could not get on with anything else whilst they seemingly scowled in his direction, and he consequently pressed a buzzer under his desk.

"What is it?" The Inspector appearing round the door seemed none too pleased at being summoned believing that he was fully entitled to take some time away from his chores and sit with his feet up for a while. For her part Jayne now felt exhilarated that they had decided to wait for she had been convinced that the man whom they sought had been on the premises all of the time. Still for his part now noticing who was waiting for him in the outer office the Inspector gave a sigh as if he considered his mortal life to now be in some sort of danger. "Oh it is you two is it? Well I suppose you had better come inside!" The later words were spoken almost begrudgingly much to Jayne's surprise although Luc with his demeanour almost looked as if he had expected such a reception. In fact she was convinced he whispered as much as they dutifully followed the Officer to his inner sanctum.

"Perhaps you will be now good enough to tell me what this is all about considering that you have already demoted my desk sergeant into some meaningless wretch!" The Inspector remained standing. No doubt he desired this meeting to reach a conclusion very quickly

"I believe we may have met the man who was murdered close to the port quite recently!"

"And whatever gives you that idea?" At the time the Inspector held little interest in this conversation for after all as yet few details of the victim had been released to the press so such a statement made little sense to his authoritarian mind.

"If you do happen to have a photograph of the victim we would be able to either confirm or deny this meeting!" Luc paid little heed to the Inspector's question and the other man, still anxious for them to leave, sighed before producing such a likeness, for to his mind there was no secret in this and besides he expected them to now say they had been mistaken, apologise and then leave.

"It is him. My hunch was right!" The Inspector's attention was now focussed still against his will on Jayne as he wondered how this one apparently appeared to be mixed up in everything that happened to be going. "This was the person who actually passed me that parcel on the promenade. You said at the time that he was not from the ship but the other day we actually met him and when we questioned him he said that he had obtained such a parcel as well as his instructions from someone off one of the fishing boats. I know it sounds a rather far-fetched story but according to what we were told, apparently there is quite a lucrative trade in goods being brought ashore in such a manner and as it happened to be this poor wretches' day off, the naval rating was not for forfeiting earning some extra cash by working in this manner!"

"Perhaps you had better sit down after all!" The Inspector had suddenly begun to pay the pair at least partial attention. "I suppose you do not mind if I record this conversation?"

Jayne nodded her assent without waiting for Luc to be forthcoming for after all she felt that there was little else she could do under the circumstances and therefore she watched as the policeman fumbled with his apparatus before seemingly being satisfied that the recorder was in working order.

"Exactly where did you meet this fellow, why where you there at the time and what exactly did you hope to gain by such a meeting?"

"I actually wanted to know what had happened to my mother's ashes!" By this time Luc had decided it was time to interject and consequently the Inspector looked scathingly in Luc's direction as if wondering whether taking such a recording would prove to be of any use to anyone before he turned his attention back onto Jayne possibly wondering whether this one would make more sense in what she had to say!

"Initially I had to do some shopping and it was whilst I was carrying out my quest that I became convinced that I caught sight of the man you seemed to refuse to believe existed. I mentioned the sighting to Luc here and as the mysterious man was a sailor after some discussion we felt that we had a better chance of backing up this sighting around the port area itself, and consequently it was on the road outside of the place that we actually spotted him. Perhaps the man was as perplexed as what we were at this meeting but then after questioning him we discovered that he had indeed brought the parcel from the fishing vessel that night, which was probably the reason why you could find no sign of him on the ferry boat itself when you investigated"

"So you are trying to say that this fellow came ashore from the fishing vessel then?" The Inspector's eyes widened as he began to try to distinguish between the truth and fiction in this woman's ramblings

"That is what he told us. He said that he came ashore to deliver the parcel to me as had been previously arranged, the only difference being that this parcel had supposedly been deftly extricated from the ferry boat and onto the fishing vessel for some apparent reason!"

"We have indeed already checked with our French counterparts and the undertakers in question and such a packet, supposedly containing your mother's ashes was indeed loaded onto the vessel in Calais to be collected at Dover by a courier!"

"So what then happened to my mother's ashes? I can assure you that they were not coated with some ridiculous product like the one you discovered in the parcel when you decided to open it!"

"According to the naval rating to whom we spoke, his theory was that once the parcel had been passed to the fishing boat then the ashes were substituted for the unlawful product that you managed to find Inspector. This was the parcel that I was indeed expected to collect and then deliver to Mr Mathieu!" Jayne ignored Luc's persistent questioning as she made to conclude her own theory on the matter.

"Yes!" It now appeared to be the Inspector's turn to stroke his chin thoughtfully. "Strangely enough it also appears that your story is to some extent backed up by our colleagues in France. Yet I now have a question for you Mr Mathieu, when did you last see your father?"

Jayne watched as the blood rushed to Luc's face and wondered for a moment whether he would deem to reply to such a question under the circumstances for the switch from thinking about the whereabouts of his mother's missing ashes to dwell on his father seemed to be a great deal to expect from the man.

"Not since I was a mere babe or so I am told and therefore I cannot say that I have any recollection of the man!" Jayne was somewhat surprised at how well Luc appeared to handle the situation

"And yet Jules Mathieu is reported to have been a passenger on that ferry. That is your father's name I presume Mr Mathieu?"

"I believe he was called by that name. At least that is the name written on my birth certificate. But I am afraid that is all that I know about this person. I would not know him even if I met him and I don't suppose he would know me either!"

"Then if perchance you should come into contact with him Mr Mathieu perhaps you will contact us!" The Inspector stood; obviously he considered the interview was now at an end. The recorder switched off he motioned his guests towards the door. "I will arrange for a transcript of the recording to be typed out and then perhaps you will sign it Mr Mathieu!"

"You want me to sign it now?" Luc was not sure what he was supposed to do.

"I think you must allow us a little time Mr Mathieu to prepare the same. I will require both of you to sign the document of course as being a true recording of our meeting, but perhaps you can call back either later today or tomorrow!" The policeman now seemed to be anxious to get rid of them. Not that Luc felt very pleased about the prospect of having to return to this place at a later stage but then they were in no position to argue. For her part Jayne remained silent, perhaps she was indeed looking towards Luc for some inspiration by this time.

"Well I suppose that means we will have to come back, but not today thank you. We will call after I have been to collect the results of my D.N.A. testing!" At least she supposed he had made a decision and one that she was willing to abide by

They rode back to Priory Manor in silence for Luc's thoughts were obviously far away. Jayne did not question although she wondered if these thoughts were now centred on the father he had never known. Altogether his family life appeared to speak of tragedy. Still unwilling to pry, for after all it really was none of her business, once back at the Hall she sought to occupy herself in the house, much to Mrs Bentham's consternation, for the woman, still in mourning for the deceased, believed that all should be left exactly the way it was almost indeed like some cherished mausoleum.

It was therefore much to Mrs Bentham's pleasure when the doorbell rang and upon answering it she found a person asking for Jayne by name, for to the housekeeper's mind anything that would divert the girl away from upsetting the household must be a good thing. Consequently the woman never even queried this caller's purpose, a factor that could be said to be most unusual for this female who picture herself as some sort of custodian both of the place and its inmates and normally would have deemed to halt any disturbance of their privacy. Jayne however, answering the call to the front door experienced something of a shock when she saw Simon standing there.

"Your mother said that you would be in need of these!" He pushed the case he was carrying forward intending this to be an opening and one that Jayne would anxiously clasp. "As a matter of fact the woman is worried out of her mind about you as are we all. What is going on Jayne?" He was obviously expecting to be admitted and therefore Jayne could do little else but allow him into the hallway. "What are you doing here anyway?" She wondered as she glanced at his expression whether his eyes were roving around the place in admiration or in preparation to make some criticism.

"I thought that I had already explained that at the moment I am unable to leave the area!" Jayne did not know why she felt glad that Luc was out at the time and therefore could not see her flushed expression.

"Your mother mentioned something about the police. I must admit that I was horrified when she told me that you had been involved with them for just imagine what that sort of news could do to my reputation!"

"Not to mention what spending a night in a police cell did to me!" It was typically like Simon to always be thinking of his own position, she reflected. In fact Simon was always like that in putting his own situation the first to be considered.

"I understood that was all a big mistake so now that they have let you go why is it that you cannot come back home?"

"I thought that I had already explained, I am not yet allowed to leave the area whilst the police investigations are on-going!"

"But you mentioned the area in question in general terms therefore what are you doing at this place?"

"Without either clothes or money at the time I was only too thankful to find a friend who took pity on me!" Jayne knew that his eyes widened but at the time she didn't care, Simon was prone not to even consider such matters.

"Then if as you say it was money that you needed why did you not contact me? Also why on earth were you careering around on your brother's motorbike at the time? I consider that to be most unladylike and besides if you had not been doing so then you would not have ended up in this mess!"

"Because having recently found myself unemployed I happened to take a job as a courier and couriers are expected to do that sort of thing in order to deliver parcels and documents speedily. As I did not expect to be staying for long in the area my mission being only to collect a parcel from off the ferry and then deliver it here I omitted to bring a change of clothes with me which I must agree was most negligent of me!"

"Yet you seem to have obtained a change of clothes now!" Perhaps he had still expected to see her clad in her riding gear for that to Simon would have been black and white and the man normally refused to see any shades of grey in his argument.

"I was lent the money by my new friend!" Jayne wondered why she had never been defiant to Simon before. She supposed she had always been something of a 'yes' person with him mainly because this had usually proved to be the easier way out of a situation.

"In that case you must give the money back immediately!" Simon was already fishing for his wallet for to Simon money always provided the solution to a situation. "And whilst you are at it you had better also pay this person for your board and lodgings. I will arrange for you to stay somewhere in the town for I am sure that would be far more prudent than staying in the same premises as a man!"

"Now why would you want to do that?" Jayne felt herself catch a breath at these words for she had not heard Luc return. Now turning her head she saw him standing nonchalantly by the door as if he was weighing up the situation and furthermore had taken something of a dislike to his visitor.

"Simon brought some clothes for me from home!" Perhaps at a loss at what to say Jayne indicated the suitcase which was now stood rather forlornly in the hallway and wished with all of her heart that neither Simon nor the dratted suitcase was here.

"How perfectly thoughtful of him and no doubt he was querying your present position?" She could have sworn that Luc was now enjoying this situation and possibly anxious to see her squirm.

"Simon happens to work at the headquarters of a bank and he is also a friend of the family!" She offered the knowledge as a way of finding something to say and at the same time wondered why she still felt reluctant to tell Luc the truth although in the event she did not have to wait for long before it was wrested from her lips.

"Jayne and I also happen to be engaged!" Perhaps it was now the sheer arrogance on the man's face when he spoke that promoted Luc to retaliate.

"Now is that a fact. But I do not see any ring on Jayne's finger. Surely as a banker that must have been one item you could have afforded!" Luc had picked up her hand in the pretence of examining it much to the annoyance of the other man.

"Perhaps that is none of your business Mr -----!"

"Mathieu is the name. Did Jayne fail to relay that in her phone message?"

"I have no doubt Mr Mathieu that Jayne owes you a debt of gratitude but now I must insist that she recompenses you for your expenditure and that I find her alternative accommodation for after all it cannot be considered proper for the girl to stay here!"

"I am afraid that is not possible Mr –err Banker for you see she is required by the police to stay at this address, at least for the foreseeable future. To do otherwise would no doubt ensure the rage of the law and I am sure that you would not wish to see her taken into custody again for she spent a rather miserable night there before!"

"In that case perhaps you will excuse us so that I might have a conversation with my fiancé?"

"There is plenty of room for such a conference in the grounds of the Manor. No doubt you witnessed how extensive they were when you drove in!" And so saying Luc made to move inside. Perhaps at the time Jayne failed to see the expression on his face but her own thoughts now seemed to be tangled up in some precipitous whirlpool. For his part Simon let him go before motioning her to follow him outside for as far as he was concerned if this was what the owner of this place dictated and therefore under the circumstances they were forced to oblige.

"You still have a great deal of explaining to do Jayne. In fact you have no idea how that phone call to your mother affected the woman. In fact to hear that her daughter has not only been in trouble with the police but is now living in some country manor with a person who does not even appear to be of British descent is enough to make any mother brim with anxiety. Other than that your phone call was so short that she could not make any sense out of the matter. Therefore you can imagine my surprise when she came to me for assistance. Not that the fact, if it ever came out that my fiancé had been in trouble with the police would prove to be of any assistance in my own career cannot be underestimated either!"

"For a start can we can one or two things straight Simon? First of all I am not officially your fiancé or anything else despite what you claim therefore I cannot see how this business could possibly affect your career and secondly although I thank my mother for sending me my clothes I have no intention to move from Priory Manor at this moment in time and neither is Luc Mathieu the foreigner you purport him to be. The fact that we found ourselves mixed up in this affair together is something only fully known to some sort of fate. Therefore although I probably must thank you for coming down here to ascertain that I am all right I can assure you that is the case and therefore you can return back and tell my mother so!" Jayne surprised herself with her rendering and perhaps wondered why she had never been so forthright before for if she had been then Simon

Turnbill would not be left under any illusion that she was his fiancée. She wondered why that fact above all others served to irritate her now for previously she had apparently been quite content to sit back and allow him to do all the organising, unless, she reminded herself, she had seen this as being the easy way out.

"I am staying at the Red Lion close by tonight therefore if you have further thoughts on the matter and decide to do the sensible thing you can contact me there before I leave in the morning. I must add that it has been most inconvenient for me to have to take time off work as it is and therefore I find your present attitude to be most disconcerting!"

He stayed no longer and Jayne watched him go with a feeling of relief. It was a relief however that was to be short lived when she entered the Hall to be confronted with Luc.

"So it was a lie you told me when you said that you had no commitments all of which makes me wonder just how many more lies you have told me of late!"

"The fact that Simon decided to make far more out of our relationship than what really existed was hardly a lie. In fact I do not pretend to go around telling such untruths!"

She watched as perhaps still unconvinced by her argument Luc gripped his knuckles before moving off into another part of the house and suddenly for no apparent reason she felt rather sad.

★ ★ ★

It was Mrs Bentham who unwittingly served to break the impasse between them after summonsing them to the evening meal. Not that the woman had any intention of bringing the two of them together, far from it, for she was more concerned with an observation she had made even whilst the other two regarded each other as if daggers were drawn almost ready to do battle.

"Guess there was a stranger around these parts earlier on in the day!" Her words were uttered in the hopes of receiving some explanation of this sighting for Mrs Bentham did not go a bundle on unsolved mysteries.

"No doubt you are meaning Miss Taylor's friend?" The words from Luc were issued with some irony which at any other time Jayne could easily have challenged for the tonality of them sounded as if they had been spat from his lips.

"No I am not referring to that positive excuse for humanity although I would much prefer it if he remained a stranger around here. No, there was someone else who was snooping in the grounds. I saw a shadow from the kitchen window and later the gardener backed me up by saying that he had also spotted someone!"

"No doubt a stray or else a member of the family seeing what assets he could manage to secure for himself!" Luc still sounded scathing in his tone.

"Well I would say that the man was obviously looking for something and he was not one of your so called relatives either. He must have been around for a good twenty minutes or so before he caught sight of me watching him through the window and after that he did a rapid exit!"

"So I can take it that you frightened him off?" Now looking at Luc's expression Jayne could not help the chuckles beginning to form in her throat for to her mind it sounded as though Luc was suggesting that it was the sight of Mrs Bentham's face that had frightened the intruder away.

"All I said is that the man, whoever he happened to be, went away!" Mrs Bentham obviously refused to be drawn on such remarks for she gave her usual audible sniff and made her exit leaving the other two alone.

"Perhaps I was a little unfair in what I said to you earlier on!" Luc shuffled his feet under the table, a sure sign that he was a little embarrassed at having to make this apology.

"It was my own fault. Perhaps I should have mentioned something about Simon before but the matter seemed irrelevant and anyway the time can hardly be considered to have been opportune! But I will say one thing and that is Simon Turnbill never was nor is he ever likely to be my fiancé even if he has read far more into our past relationship than what was good for him, no doubt obviously encouraged at the time by my parents. Maybe I should have done more to persuade him of that fact earlier on!"

"Sometimes I suppose it seems to be easier to go along with the flow. Anyway tomorrow, don't forget, we have our appointment with the Inspector to sign that statement we made which will have been duly typed out!"

"We will go only after we have been to the hospital to get your D.N.A. reading! Don't tell me that you are now getting cold feet about that now?"

"Why should I for I know exactly where I came from?"

"Yet your expression at the thought of going back to the hospital to collect your proof tells me something entirely different. Not that I for one moment think you will be let down with the result for after all you already bear the arrogance of the gentry at times!" She dodged as a bread roll came across the table in her direction. "Even to throwing your crumbs on the floor for Mrs Bentham to clear up!"

"Jayne Taylor you are an astounding girl. I am beginning to wonder now what I did before you came into my life even if I was tempted to shut the door on you on first sight!"

The D.N.A. reading collected from the hospital Luc had to return with it first in order to present the same to Edgar Withers the solicitor who occupied those dingy premises in Canterbury. Upon entering his office they found the man in a sombre state of mind, not that Luc, as he later admitted had witnessed the man being in any other. Even so the man appeared to want to express his current thoughts without prompting

"I have just been entertaining Stuart Bardon!" The mention of this name immediately riveted Luc's attention for this was the name of his second cousin, the son of

Edward Bardon's younger brother and the one who had claimed that the Hall should by rights be passed onto him. The solicitor cleared his voice before continuing. "He claims that your father is currently in this country Mr Mathieu. Under the present circumstances would you consider that to be significant?"

Jayne watched as she saw Luc's lips tense. Of course he knew well enough that, Stuart Bardon, the son of Hector Bardon, the younger brother of Edward and consequently his second cousin, would go to any length in order to discredit him to achieve his own ends, but the fact that his father was apparently in this country only served to reinforce what the Inspector had told them the previous day although as to why his father now wished to grace the shores of England was something that Luc failed to understand.

"I doubt whether I would know my biological father even if I met him face to face; therefore whether he happens to be in this country or not is really of no significance to me." Jayne decided that Luc put a brave face on when he gave his answer for she knew full well that when the Inspector had previously mentioned the matter Luc had been puzzled as to what this man had wanted. "I am here simply to provide you with my D.N.A. reading which you can check with the hospital authorities if you so wish. Maybe that document will convince both you and my meddling relatives that I am after all the true heir to my grandfather, Edward Bardon!"

The solicitor took the paper with a thoughtful expression on his face and Jayne wondered whether the man was now contemplating what he would say to Luc's relatives now that this paper had been delivered. But as there was little more to say to this man Luc made his excuses and left, their intention now to drive to see the Inspector in his enclave at the port and keep their appointment.

"And after that I will buy you lunch in Canterbury!" Luc tried to force the smile on his face as they left the rather antiquated office although in all truth the smile did not reach his eyes. To Jayne however the smile was something for at least she presumed he had pushed the meeting with Simon to the back of his mind!

Their business with the Inspector quickly completed Luc and Jayne then returned to the town and noticing that the worry lines had not been erased from his face Jayne stuck her neck out to question him.

"I was remembering what Mrs Bentham told us last night about that person she had spotted in the grounds and just wondering -----!"

"Wondering what? You must know Luc that a worry shared is a worry halved!"

He glanced at her again across the table of the restaurant where they had decided to eat and this time she was convinced that she saw some softening in his eyes.

"Maybe it sounds ridiculous but with the number of sightings there has apparently been of this man I was wondering whether it was Jules Mathieu, although why the man should want to seek me out at this time when he has had nothing to do with me since I was a baby seems to be incomprehensible!"

"Is there any reason why he might want to try to find you? For example could it be about your mother's death?"

"I cannot see that Jules Mathieu would be interested in that. I did in fact try to contact him through an intermediary following my mother's demise but he never responded and neither did he show his face at her funeral!"

"Then maybe, if it is him, he wants to apologise to you for his behaviour. Perhaps indeed he has had second thoughts for you are after all his son!"

"Nice try Jayne but unfortunately Jules does not work like that. If he has followed me here to this country then it is because he wants something!" The hardened expression had now returned to Luc's eyes and it was something that Jayne would have liked to have wiped away for after all if Luc did not know his father then he could not possibly say what the man wanted if anything at all. "You don't really believe that families can act like that, do you Jayne? But I am afraid that is a fact of life. Anyway to return to the menu!" He waved the menu in front of her almost as if he was now anxious to change the subject.

She ordered still unable to get the thought of that expression out of her mind for somehow she did not like to see Luc hurt. And then she chastised herself, whatever was she thinking about for she and Luc were only casual acquaintances thrown together by the fortunes of life. It was a temporary relationship only which must end quite soon when other matters had been cleared up and she had not got to let her heart deceive her into thinking otherwise!

Chapter Four

It was just after breakfast the following morning when Luc received a phone call saying that the solicitor wanted to see him again. In truth the phone call brought a scowl to Luc's face.

"Now what does he want?" The voice of impatience differed most markedly to the way they had conversed on the previous day for at that time they had appeared to be on the point of developing a certain relationship; but now it was sheer frustration which coloured Luc's tones. "Surely he is not blathering on about that land again!"

"What land are you talking about?" Perhaps Jayne surprised herself at the way the question now came easily to her lips.

"Oh some that was mentioned in the will!" Luc appeared to be quite disinterested in the fact; a matter that still aroused Jayne's curiosity for nothing like this had been mentioned before.

"So you now own land as well?"

"Well apparently Edward Bardon owned some land up in the North of the country. It was several acres of land that he apparently inherited from his own father and so forth. To all accounts this acreage was first purchased way back during the canal era, only my forefathers must have been disappointed with their purchase for this portion of land was not required for any canal building and therefore to all intents and purposes it has remained fallow and rented out at a peppercorn rent to some farmer ever since!"

"So why does Mr Withers want to see you about it now?"

"Goodness only knows!"

"Then I suppose the only way that you will find out is to pay him a visit!" Jayne's suggestion was made in a soft voice for she supposed that under the circumstances it was the only thing she could say.

"Then that will ruin all my secret plans that I have been busy hatching out for today: Things that we could do together. After all you have not really seen much of the area around here yet and I thought we could possibly take a drive out without having to stop in town; a drive which would not leave the area of your confinement of course!" He had fixed his eyes on her again and Jayne firmly believed that she could feel their penetrating blue colouration on her flesh.

"Still going to the solicitor's to see what he wants will hardly take all day!" She found herself searching for the right words in order to spur him on to the task which he obviously needed to complete the only trouble being that look he gave her which almost penetrated her senses.

"True enough if you will come with me!" Luc was ready with his response. In all truth he had found himself now wanting to spend every available moment with this girl and matters which served to upset this wish were not highly favoured by him.

"I'm sure that your solicitor does not want to see me and furthermore if I am there on the doorstep with you then he most probably will refrain from saying what he intended. Perhaps the best idea is for you to go there on your own and then if your mind is still set on us traversing the area then you can come back here for me afterwards!"

Luc pulled a face. The idea did not exactly please him but then he had to admit the girl spoke common sense. "Then promise me you won't disappear while I am away!"

"And where exactly do you expect me to disappear to?"

"I don't know, perhaps your old boyfriend will appear on the scene to spirit you away!"

"I can assure you that there is no chance of that happening. Anyway what have I got to do to make you understand that there is not, nor was there ever, any lasting agreement between myself and Simon!"

"All right--- All right, I will take your word for it!" At least there was a glimmer of his good humour returning. "Anyway tell Mrs Bentham that she can take the day off for she is owed some time and we won't be returning until late!" And so saying Luc disappeared, ready to make preparations to go into town.

Left on her own after his departure Jayne was toying with matters around the Hall when the doorbell rang. It was Mrs Bentham not having yet departed, who was the one to answer it and upon doing so she gave Jayne a shout to attract her attention.

"It's that policeman here to see you Miss. I told him the master was out but apparently he wants to see you!" Jayne could well imagine Mrs Bentham sniffing at the thought of a visit from the law but nevertheless she made her way to the hall whereupon the old retainer, still hoping that no one in the vicinity had witnessed the police visiting the Hall again, took pains to make a rapid exit.

"Sorry if I have disturbed you Miss Taylor but I thought I would call round in person to give you the news!" The Inspector looked expectantly at the doorstep and Jayne felt obliged to invite him inside. It seemed as if a strange situation that had been foisted upon her for after all this was not her house and therefore she felt that she should not have been the one to have invited the man inside.

"Luc I am afraid is out at the moment. He had a call to go to see his solicitor this morning!" At least this appeared to be the most reasonable thing to say under the circumstances but then the Inspector did not appear concerned about Luc's absence for the man had news to impart to this girl, a task he was eager to complete and then he could be about his own business.

"So your housekeeper said but then my business does not concern Mr Mathieu at the moment but rather yourself. The Captain of the fishing boat we spoke about earlier has now been arrested and he has confessed to both handling the parcel we found you with and also substituting the original contents of the same for alternative material. What he has not yet told us however is how the parcel managed to find its way onto the fishing boat in the first place when we have witnesses to say it was delivered to the port and even more importantly neither do we know who the person was that authorised this exchange. Neither has he told us of what became of the ashes which were contained in the box originally. Still what concerns you at the moment is, I am pleased to say, any charges against you have now been dropped and therefore you are now free to leave the area whenever you wish!"

"And what about Luc?" Jayne's thoughts immediately turned to the other, but upon her words the Inspector shook his head.

"I am sorry but at the moment Luc Mathieu seems to have been the intended recipient of this consignment of drugs and therefore until we have proof to the contrary I am afraid that he must remain on our suspect list: And now if you will excuse me Miss Taylor!"

Jayne was aware of Mrs Bentham's laudable sniffs as the Inspector took his leave for the woman had obviously not yet taken advantage of having the day off but had been listening to the conversation in some earnest. Aware that Jayne had noticed her presence however Eliza

Bentham decided to show at least some sympathetic understanding of the situation

"Guess I sometimes wonder why we bother to pay that lot. Why can't they go and catch criminals instead of bothering the likes of us!"

"I suppose they have a job to do Mrs Bentham!"

"Guess it's all right for you for to talk now for after all you have now got your freedom quite unlike the master!"

"I am sure that it is only a question of time before Mr Mathieu is also vindicated!"

"So I suppose you will now be for leaving us Miss?"

"Not exactly leaving at this moment in time for I will have to explain things to Mr Mathieu when he returns and anyway we have agreed to go out somewhere today. Why are you anxious to get rid of me then?"

The woman seemed to think for a moment. "Perhaps I am not after all for you seem to have brought a certain feeing of lightness into this place. But if you are sure you will still be here when I get back then I will be off. Guess I might as well make full use of the day whilst I have the opportunity!"

Jayne watched the woman make her way out with some thought. It was after all the first time since she arrived at the Hall that the woman had made her feel that she was welcome here. Anyway now with time to spare Jayne thought she might as well take a look at that old transport of hers which was still lying and gathering dust in one of the outhouses. At least she supposed that she could start up the engine and check if it was working all right.

She was intent upon her task so much so that she failed to spot the shadowy figure currently out in the grounds of the Hall, at least that was not until he actually confronted her. "I believe I am speaking to Miss Jayne Taylor?"

"If you are then what do you want? These happen to be private grounds so what are you doing here?" Not comfortable with this man's presence so close to the house and wondering what had made him transverse the drive Jayne attempted to put a note of authority into her voice, not that she felt anything else but uncomfortable in this man's presence

"I heard that you had spark about you!" The stranger now confronted her with a coarse laugh. Tall and yet sturdy in his appearance the expression on his face suddenly reminded her of someone she knew, and for a moment she wracked her brains trying to think who that was.

"What do you want?" Again she demanded the question off him now conscious that she was very much on her own at this place.

"A little bit of assistance Miss that is all. I believe you are acquainted with my son?"

The words shocked her as she realised that the reason his expression had led her to believe that it reminded her of someone else was indeed a truth, for this surely must be Jules Mathieu. The question was what was he doing here and why had he come here to co-opt her assistance?

"I will repeat what I said. What do you want?" Jayne forced her voice to sound tough which was far more than what she actually felt. Yet in response she suddenly felt a hand grasping hold of her wrist.

"I believe it is likely to be necessary for you to persuade my son to see the error of his ways in certain matters. With luck this should not serve to delay you for too long. I noticed that you had come here to take a look at your bike. It should be a very useful machine for you to get home on after of course you have completed the task I have in mind for you!"

"I will do no such thing!"

"Oh but I think that you will my dear!" The hold on her wrist tightened and now she realised that he was hurting her. "It was rather fortunate I think that the housekeeper was allowed to take the day off for now there is literally no one around to disturb us. Consequently I am sure that I will soon be able to make you see matters my way!" Whilst she searched her throat to produce some sort of a scream to find no sound to be forthcoming he merely laughed at her efforts. "You are wasting your time my dear for with your housekeeper away there is literally no one around the place to listen to your warbles and believe that you might need some assistance!" His tones when he spoke were ugly and Jayne shivered whilst at the same time she struggled to free herself. Yet her captor appeared to view such struggles as a challenge as he pulled her against her will away from her bike to the place where he fully intended that she would come, either voluntarily or with the use of force. A whimper crossed her lips as she spotted the waiting car and yet she knew full well that it was useless to scream for help for there was literally no one here at the present to hear such cries for assistance.

The man appeared to have the strength of some superior being for still holding onto her he managed to force open the door to that vehicle and made to thrust her inside. She heard the wails finally dissipating from her lips as they managed to find a voice for themselves and almost expected a hand to now be clamped over her lips in a fiercely fraught attack. Yet if she had been expecting a blow to herself this now appeared to come from the outside of the vehicle and it was not aimed at her but rather at the person who now held her captive.

Forcing her eyes open from their clenched position she laid eyes on her rescuer. Yet this was not Luc whom she had both hoped and anticipated that it would be but another familiar figure and someone who now grabbed her by her shoulder over the fallen form of Jules Mathieu. Neither could it be said that her rescuer was prone to issue any niceties' for she now found herself practically propelled towards another vehicle, a vehicle she had not heard enter into the precincts of the Hall and the face of the rescuer she now beheld appeared fraught with the same equal determination as what her previous captor had portrayed.

"Get in that car now!" Yet the voice which now ordered her was not unfamiliar as Simon Turnbill motioned her inside. "You are going home Jayne. Perhaps now after this sordid encounter you will be ready to agree that this place holds nothing at all for you.

Your mother is right it is obviously time for you to return home!"

When Luc Mathieu entered the offices of Eric Withers the solicitor, he was not in a particularly good mood. For starters he wanted to know just what the old man wanted this time to summon him here in this manner, for surely he had provided this person with all the documentation he had required and now Luc was wondering what the old man needed in addition to enable to tie up the matter of the will which to his mind should have been already completed and was consequently overdue! This accompanied by the fact that the trip into town had used up time he would far rather have spent with Jayne, for let us face it he was beginning to covet the girl's company, convinced Luc that it would have placed anyone in a rather darkened mood as they made for those offices.

Neither could it be said that the man, although obviously expecting him to answer his call without delay, was not all that overjoyed to see him for he adopted the irritating fashion of tidying up his paper clips in the tray on his desk before bothering to even look in Luc's direction. It was indeed only when the silence became unbearable and Luc was on the point of issuing forth a mouthful of abuse that the solicitor decided to state his case.

"I am afraid that I have some news for you Mr Mathieu, rather unfortunate news in a manner of speaking for you see Mr Stuart Bardon a close relative of yours has recently been to see me and what he told me I found to be quite frankly most disturbing. Apparently the man has it on good authority Mr Mathieu that you yourself are a changeling. By that I mean that the person you knew of as your mother was not your biological parent at all, which of course if correct will alter the context of the will in which you were to inherit the estate by right of birth!"

"Whatever nonsense is this?" Perhaps Luc did not fully understand the implications at this stage. "I thought I provided a D.N.A. sample to prove my lineage as I was requested so to do?"

"That of course will be taken into consideration as will the evidence that Mr Bardon now has to put before us!"

"I am afraid that I do not appreciate your thinking Mr Withers!" Luc tried to disguise the feeling that had now stolen over him. He had obliged by fulfilling what had been required of him not expecting such an outcome which now quite frankly served to bewilder him.

"I have no doubt that my words have come as something of a shock to you Mr Mathieu. Nevertheless it is imperative that all options should be fully investigated in matters such as this and therefore all such evidence gleaned must be put before a higher authority whose decision on the matter must be abided by! In other words Mr Mathieu any such decisions concerning the legitimacy of such claims can no longer be made by this office!"

"And what if I was to say that I hold strong objections to your own words when you used the word changeling when you spoke of my mother?"

"I report the facts or otherwise as they are related to me. Perhaps it is therefore one matter you could take up with counsel when they meet to discuss your case. And now as I am a very busy man I will say good day to you Mr Mathieu!"

This seemed to be the end of all fruitful conversation with this man lamented Luc for now it appeared that his future was to be decided by some counsel. No doubt his relative would now be beaming at the thought although how this person has managed to obtain some false information regarding his parentage and why the D.N. A. result was now proving to be of no consequence seemed to be beyond him. Yet this was obviously not the place to ask further questions and his mind turned back onto Jayne. At least he had someone there who was prepared to listen to him and might possibly be able to suggest some action he could follow to him. Therefore there was now only one place where he could go and the thought of Jayne at least did something to calm the savage beast that now lay within him because of the injustice which had been currently served to him!

"But where has she gone?" It was Mrs Bentham who was to bear the brunt of Luc's voice concerning Jayne's absence when she finally returned back to the Hall for by this time Luc had forgotten that he had told the woman to take the day off.

"Of that I have no idea Sir. All I can say is that the lass was in the place when I left earlier. In fact if you remember rightly she was waiting for you to return from your appointment for you had spoken about going out for the day and to my mind the lass was looking forward to it!" It was a staunch reminder to him for Mrs Bentham was quite good at issuing such matters when the need arose and sometimes it was very necessary to remind a man of promises he had made earlier.

"So you have no idea where she has gone?" He was conscious that Mrs Bentham was showing some surprise at his persistence in this matter.

"No although before I left the Hall the girl had a visit from that Inspector. As a matter of fact he told her that she was free to go if she so wished but she definitely said that she was waiting for you to return!" The housekeeper watched as Luc drummed his fist down on a nearby table. Acting in that manner almost made her think he was sweet on the girl but then she supposed in life things seldom worked out as one had planned. "Who knows though perhaps she did change her mind after all and decided that she would go home, maybe she was missing her folk!" There were things that she had to see to and talking to the master like this was hardly getting them finished. "Perhaps you should try and contact her back where she came from. I suppose you know her home address?"

Luc shook his head. She had spoken about her parents, she had even contacted her mother when she had first arrived here but he did not know her address. Perhaps it was fortuitous that he suddenly remembered the telephone she had used and the fact that it did retain several of the last call numbers. Well that particular telephone had not been used much since Jayne had phoned home so perhaps there was just a chance the number would still be recorded. That was when he wasted no further time before going to look for it!

There could be little doubt that anger showed in Simon's eyes as he endeavoured to steer the car in a more Northerly direction and his accompanying silence was almost as cutting as any words he could have uttered could have proved to be. Yet for Jayne, once she had recovered from the trauma which had beset her before they had left the Hall, such a silence was not enough, yet they had almost reached Birmingham before she found the words to break into this impasse.

"How did you find me?" Surely he must respond to her question.

"That was the easy part. You phoned your mother remember and a little detective work on my part happened to trace the call. But now perhaps it is my turn. First of all who was that man whom I caught trying to accost you back there and perhaps more importantly what the hell where you doing at that place anyway? It may be of some interest to you to know that your mother has been frantic since your disappearance. She didn't particularly approve of you taking the job of a courier in the first place but she hardly expected you to take up residence down there at that place. Consequently I felt forced into taking some valuable time off my work simply to come and collect you and therefore I must tell you that I consider your actions to have bordered on the absurd!"

Well she supposed she had at least succeeded in making him speak to her although she determined that her answer to his question would come in small doses.

"The person you saw happened to be Luc's estranged father, at least I have reason to believe it was!"

"And who the hell is Luc then?"

"Luc is the person to whom I was supposed to deliver the parcel to as part of the courier service. Unfortunately things did not work out according to plan. I was supposed to be delivering a parcel containing his mother's ashes, but instead I found myself with a parcel of narcotics!" She heard Simon's gasp on the word narcotics and half smiled to herself. Of course with his well-ordered life matters of this course never entered to disturb it and to even hear about such things obviously shocked him.

"You were delivering narcotics? Am I hearing right girl?"

"You are, but what the parcel contained I had no knowledge of at the time. Unfortunately or otherwise the police intervened and as a result I was unable to leave the area. Without money and my bike temporarily confiscated I had to depend upon the kind auspices of Luc and his housekeeper and as Luc had similarly been duped with the contents of this parcel it seemed to be reasonable enough for me to stay there whilst the police continued their enquiries!"

"To me the whole thing sounds like some elaborate fairy story. I must say that I am shocked by your behaviour Jayne and no doubt you will have quite a lot of explaining to do to your mother. But let us get back to this man whom you say attacked you: if this indeed was this Luc's father why did he want to do that?"

"I'm afraid that I don't know except the man said it was to make Luc see the error of his ways!" Once again she witnessed the look of abject horror on Simon's face as she uttered her response. But it was the truth after all for she had no idea what had mitigated the man to do such a thing although she did know of the bad blood that existed between father and son.

"Perhaps we should put an end to these fabrications. We will take a convenience stop before we traverse the outskirts of Birmingham and after that we will drive you straight home. As our conversation is nothing if not confusing perhaps we should desist from further exchanges until you are in a better frame of mind!"

She wondered if Simon had thought that she might try to do a runner when he stopped the car for the man seemed to wait outside of the Ladies convenience until she reappeared and then hustled her back again to the car and after that, silence ensued!

There could be little doubt that Mrs Taylor was pleased to see her daughter even if she was still a little perplexed in the manner by which she had arrived home. In truth the woman had always felt a little uneasy when she was in the presence of SimonTurnbill. Not that there was anything wrong with the boy, far from it, she simply got the impression that this young man, a banker who commuted daily to Manchester for his employ, always seemed to have the habit of looking down his nose at her own modest surrounds. There was no doubt that this young man would have proved to be a catch for any young woman and her Jayne had always been the one he had shown an interest in. Indeed he must have otherwise he would not have frequented the house which he considered to be poor by his standards as often as what he did and it would have been wrong for her to have speculated that her Jayne could have done any better than encourage his attention. But then her daughter had always been known to be strong willed for although she may have been without a job it had been hardly fitting for her to have taken that job as a courier and to have gone charging off on her brother's motor bike all over the country the way that she had!

Simon, of course now deserved her undying gratitude for bringing Jayne home, not really words which she could convey to one elegant young bachelor and thus she took the opportunity to round on her daughter in an attempt to discover exactly what had been going on. Perhaps Simon for his part had realised her intentions and most probably had timed his exit promptly by saying that the two of them now needed to spend some time together and of course at the time she had never seen the expression on Simon's face, for this one's only desire now having brought Jayne home, was to exit the house he disapproved of by promising to call back later.

"So where on earth have you been? I knew full well that no good would come out of you charging off on your brother's bike like that. Don't you realise how worried we have been about you ever since we got that mumbled phone call from you that did not appear to make sense to us at all?"

"I thought you understood Mum. There was a misunderstanding with the police and I was therefore unable to leave the county. As I had no money on me at the time, let alone clothes so that I could get out of those leathers I guess I was fortunate to find Luc Mathieu. Well actually I didn't so much find him for he happened to be mixed up in the whole silly fiasco and therefore it was the police who found him for me, but he did have a large mansion in those parts and a housekeeper as well, before you get any silly ideas, and as far as the police were concerned it was ideal for me to stay there on a temporary basis!"

"But this temporary basis hardly appeared to be temporary did it?"

"Strange as it may sound to you Mum I was only given my clearance by the police a short time before Simon arrived. How did he manage to find me anyway?"

"He traced you from that phone call you made. Simon is clever about things like that! Really you ought to try to cultivate that young man more instead of setting out to shock him all the time!" Her mother was obviously more in favour with Simon's tactics than her own therefore Jayne decided that is was probably better not to extend the conversation further at the present time. "And what about your brother's motor bike that you went careering off on? Apparently Robert's regiment is due to return to the U.K. next week and when he returns home I don't suppose he will be overjoyed to learn that his bike is now in foreign places!"

"Not foreign places Mum. As a matter of fact it is currently locked away in one of Luc's sheds. Under the circumstances I didn't consider it advisable to ask Simon to bring it back home for me even if he could have managed to transport it in his car. After all it might possible have marked his upholstery!"

"I thought you said the bike had been impounded?"

"Initially I was not able to use it if that is what you have in mind but now I have been cleared by the police retrieving it should present little problems. In fact I was intending to turn the engine over when Simon arrived!" She omitted to say anything about her entanglement with the other man for up until now she had really not come to terms as to why he had signalled her out. Again the thought of him having touched her sent shivers up her spine but fortunately her mother did not seem to notice this.

"Well I am sure that I don't know what Robert will have to say about it when he comes home on leave!"

By this time Jayne had convinced herself that she had heard quite enough and the thought of now escaping upstairs stirred her actions thus leaving her mother feeling quite exasperated with the situation. Unfortunately it was whilst she was upstairs and trying to focus her mind as what to do next that Luc rang and of course it was her mother who answered the phone.

"Yes Jayne has arrived home thanks to her boyfriend Simon who went out of his way to call at your place to collect her. No, at the moment I do not consider her to be in the right frame of mind to speak to anyone and anyway she has gone to lie down after the trauma she has been put through over recent days. Yes I will tell her that you rang but at the moment I am unwilling to disturb her.!" Elaine Taylor had no such plans to inform her daughter of this call even before she replaced the receiver for as far as she was concerned what had happened as a result of that ill-fated courier trip was far better forgotten. Perhaps Jayne could indeed be persuaded to look at Simon Turnbill through more favourable eyes!

Anxious to escape from the on-going tribunal on the home front, Jayne upon rising the next morning decided that a walk around the local area might help to clear her head, for in truth the girl had not slept much, perhaps indeed she had expected Luc to have rung her to find out what was happening and for her part her mother was not prepared to enlighten her that there had already been such a call. She smiled as she left the house for the property in the village of Esprick, whilst sufficient for their needs, hardly matched up in size or prestige to Priory Manor. But what, she demanded of herself, was she now thinking about, for her slight sojourn at the Manor was now well and truly over with?

Wandering down the lane which led onto the main road which linked the two neighbouring towns, it was then that she noticed some workmen in one of the nearby fields. Not the ordinary sort of workmen one would expect to see on farm land for this work force were wearing steel helmets and appeared to be equipped with scaffolding poles of some description. Her natural curiosity aroused, for such a sight was to say the least unusual, Jayne crossed the road in order to speak to them for in her part of the world this was quite a natural reaction in order to satisfy ones curiosity.

"Guess we are in something of a hold up at the moment Miss. As you have probably heard the presence of shale gas has been discovered in this place. What is more after a great deal of huffing and puffing from the locals we have also been granted permission to start to drill for the gas here. The only fly in the ointment is however that before we can commence we need to get the landowners permission and although he has been traced he apparently came about this area quite recently and still has some opposition to his true ownership. So until the legal beavers have made up their mind as to what belongs to who we have been left in limbo so as to speak!"

"Shale gas?" The words intrigued her and to be perfectly honest she did not understand the significance of what she had just been told.

"Yes apparently this whole area is rich in the gas which can be forced up through the rocks below the surface. In fat they do say that there will be enough gas down there to make Britain self-sufficient for forty years or more so that she will not be totally reliant on importing the stuff and therefore could help to curb the user's fuel prices in the short term at a time when the consumer is finding it very difficult to absorb increasing tariffs in the recession!"

His words left Jayne in deep thought. Employment was scarce in the area where she lived and the idea that this exploratory venture could have provided jobs in the local area and yet the project could not proceed made her feel a little morose and she was tempted to ask questions on her return home.

"To tell the truth I'm not exactly sure whether I am glad or sorry that this job is being held up!" So her mother had apparently heard about it, but then of course she would have being situated so close to the project. "At the moment I rather value the solitude we have around this place. What would happen to that if we had a works situated on the doorstep doesn't really bear thinking about. Oh by the way Simon rang, he is coming round tonight once he finishes work which after your behavioural lapse I consider to be extremely good of him. Therefore will you please try to be nice to the guy for a change?"

Jayne was surprised and not a little downcast at the thought for Simon was someone she could well have done without at this time. Still to please her mother she nodded and decided to make the most out of the situation.

In truth Simon appeared to have regained a little of his charm although strangely enough it appeared to be this same shale gas venture that he wished to talk about.

"An old friend contacted me today. In fact I haven't seen the bloke since we were at University together. Anyway he wanted to know how the project was proceeding, said he knew that there had been some problem over the land ownership but that was now well on the way to being resolved. He seemed to be anxious to come up here when things started up there, can't think why; anyway no doubt he will be able to explain more when he comes to the area!"

"And when is this friend of yours supposed to be coming then?" It was Elaine Taylor who expressed her curiosity.

"Don't know exactly when, soon I think but he said he would contact me knowing that I am local before he came! Anyway what I really came to see you about Jayne is that the Opera is coming to the theatre in town and I suggest that I get hold of two tickets for us to go!"

"That will be nice!" Jayne didn't really mean her words but then her mother was currently preening herself firmly believing that perhaps there was a chance of the two of them getting back together again.

"In that case I will get two tickets in the dress circle whilst they still have some decent ones left. After all it will be something for you to look forward to!" At least she supposed he didn't seem to stop for long that night for which Jayne was truly thankful even if her mother would have liked to have fussed over the bloke for a little longer.

"Our Robert is coming home next week. The regiment is coming back for they have finished their duty span out there!" Was her mother really trying to delay Simon from going, Jayne wondered?

"No doubt you will be relieved about to have him home under the circumstances!" She supposed Simon had to manifest the niceties before he left although what he meant by the circumstances she didn't know for after all Robert was a soldier and he had enlisted whatever circumstances had ensued. Not that she believed Simon had ever met her brother and she idly wondered what Robert would make out of him when they did, all of which served to remind her about that motorbike again. Well there was no way by which she could go down to Canterbury and collect it for herself. Plus the fact if she did have the means to get there it was quite likely that Luc would be none too pleased to see her for to her mind he hadn't tried to ring her. Maybe after all he was relieved to have seen the back of her!

Jayne was in fact relieved when Robert finally did arrive home for at least this factor appeared to take the onus away from herself and Simon. Still after his mother had finished fussing over him it seemed inevitable that Robert would go in search of his bike for in the past he had been a keen motorcyclist.

"So what is all this about?" Of course her mother had been at pains to tell him that the disappearance of his precious bike was due entirely to his sister. Whereupon Jayne was committed to recite the tale of herself taking up the mantle of a courier, not to mention what had ensued as a result of this.

Much to her surprise Robert guffawed loudly as she completed her tale and Jayne was at a loss to know whether this was because she had actually rode the bike down to the south of England, although he did know from the past that she was quite capable of this; or whether it amused him that she had found herself in trouble with the police.

"So where is the bike now?" At least he managed to contain his laughter long enough to pose the pertinent question.

"As far as I know it is still at Priory Manor. Simon had no intention of letting me ride it back here!"

"In that case if you phone that fellow you met down there we will go and collect it!" To Robert the solution seemed to be simple.

"I don't think Simon would totally approve!" She didn't know why she kept throwing Simon's name into the equation because quite frankly she didn't really care whether she offended Simon or not. Indeed Robert's suggestion would be one way by which she could legitimately distance herself from that man for a time. On the other hand returning to Priory Manor would ultimately mean she would see Luc again and as far as she knew he had never bothered to try and contact her since she left.

"I couldn't care less what Simon has to say about the idea: If you are that fond of riding then I will hire another bike and you can ride down pillion and then bring that one back on your own whilst I motor back on the other. I suppose it is still in working order?"

"I didn't wreck it up if that is what you mean!"

"Then it is settled. You ring up and make matters right with your friend and I'll tell Mum that we will leave tomorrow!" The problem now solved at least in his own mind Robert turned away to concentrate on something else thus leaving Jayne in an unenviable position of both wanting and not wanting to ring Luc up both at the same time!

Chapter Five

Luc Mathieu realised that there was something different about the Inspector's demeanour upon first setting eyes on him. Mrs Bentham had been at great pains to inform him that the man had arrived at the Hall but then he surmised that the housekeeper had adopted a mantle of protection over him since Jayne had left the place. Thinking of Jayne once again seemed to tear at his heart for he still had no idea why she had decided to leave and perhaps more importantly why she had refused to answer his phone calls, for in fact he had begun to believe that there had been a certain something developing between him and the girl who had entered his life complete with a certain motor bike.

Thus, upon Mrs Bentham's insistence, he had gone to receive the Inspector in the study still wondering what this visit was all about when he had realised that there appeared to be something entirely different in the man's attitude that day.

"It is but a fleeting visit Sir, but one which I am sure you will welcome!" Luc wondered why the man had now to preen himself before he made to continue with his rhetoric and he wondered also why he should indeed welcome a visit from the police! "Certain information which we now have at our disposal now permits me to say that although your name still remains on our suspect list as one being willing to receive contraband goods, such restrictions as those imposed appertaining to your travel in this country have now been removed although I insist that at the present time you do not make any effort to leave the country!" The Inspector looked pleased with his delivery, so pleased in fact that Luc could have been forgiven if he had believed that the man had come here to acquaint him with the fact that he had now won on the lottery!

"So I presume you have made the journey here simply to inform me of this when it appears feasible that a phone call would have sufficed?" In truth Luc discarded the policeman's pretentious enthusiasm for he was awaiting some sting to appear in the tail of this declaration.

"Maybe there still are some questions!" The Inspector looked a little flummoxed in his response, perhaps indeed Luc had caught him unaware with his declaration.

"But of course there usually are Inspector therefore do not let me hold you up from asking what you will!" For his part the Inspector now wondered if such remarks had been passed deliberately, but the man had still a job which he needed to complete.

"Have you seen your father Jules Mathieu recently Sir?" The question it appeared was intended to be aimed straight at the jugular but then of course the Inspector had perhaps had enough of the other's frivolity even if the question did bring a half smile to Luc's face.

"If I have then I am afraid that I have no knowledge of the matter. Indeed I presumed that I had previously made my position clear, I would not know my father even if we came face to face!" Quite frankly the question now served to annoy Luc. How much convincing did this man need before he finally realised that Luc had not seen his father since birth?

Perhaps the Inspector, now realising that he had strayed into the realms of repetition, allowed his tone to soften a little. "But if perchance in the future you should run into this individual then perhaps you will kindly let us know?"

"Tell me Inspector then if I was to meet this person who is apparently claiming to be my father, first of all how am I supposed to recognise him and secondly and possibly more importantly why it is important for you to know?"

The Inspector sighed possibly wondering if he was exceeding police business to speak further on this matter but then quickly decided that if he was to receive any co-operation from the man in front of him then he needed to be provided with more detail. "The man called Jules Mathieu crossed from Calais on the same ferry boat that was initially supposed to be transporting your mother's ashes to this country. We have obtained this information from our opposite number in France who received this knowledge from the undertaker responsible for transporting your mother's remains to the port. Indeed it appeared that Jules Mathieu was most anxious to travel across to this country on the same ferry boat as that container. Of course for his part the undertaker thought little at the time on this matter for he presumed it was only natural for this person to express a desire to travel alongside of the remains of his spouse. Nevertheless the French police, probing further into the matter, then discovered that Jules Mathieu's motivation to cross to this country was not solely to accompany his wife. Furthermore on further questioning the captain of the fishing boat has now admitted that he fully expected a parcel to be off loaded from that ferry boat and the person who actually dispatched it from that vessel was none other than Jules Mathieu himself!" The Inspector paused to draw breath knowing full well from the gasp of astonishment which issued forth from Luc's lips that the surprise was his and that the younger Mathieu had certainly no knowledge of this matter. "Therefore it stands to reason that we would now like to question your father on the rationale behind these actions and we strongly suspect that the man will try to contact you in the not so distant future, hence our request!" The Inspector paused again in an effort to allow his words to sink in and then noticing something or somebody was absent at the time from the Hall, pitched his next question in a more matter of fact manner.

"The young lady who was staying here with you, she appears to have left?"

"Jayne decided to go back home!" Luc was not prepared to go into the matter any further. After all as far as the police were concerned Jayne had been free to leave and therefore her reasons for doing so could hardly have been of much importance to the constabulary.

"I thought I heard something about a young man coming for her?" Ah so now the Inspector was attempting to get to the crux of the matter.

"Her fiancé I believe!" Luc now wanted this conversation to end. He did not want to be reminded of Jayne for even he could not understand what had promoted her to go off like that without saying anything!"

"That seems to be such a pity. I actually thought the two of you made quite an indomitable force together!" The Inspector made some effort now to leave for he had established what he had set out to do and now he had no wish to run into the other woman who resided at the Hall, the Housekeeper of that place, for that one appeared to be quite capable of even disorientating a man of the law.

The drive down to Priory Manor had proved to be smooth and uneventful. Fortunately the two of them had set off early enough that morning to escape any questions that would have most definitely have issued forth from Elaine Taylor's lips. Yet the closer they got to their destination the more uneasy Jayne began to feel, for she realised that Robert was still under the impression that she had phoned Luc to let him know that they were coming, but much as she would have liked to have spoken with Luc and acquaint him with the facts, Jayne chickened out of the very thought. After all in all truth she was still unaware that Luc had telephoned her mother when she had first disappeared and instead she believed that he must have thought her presence at the Hall to have been a nuisance in the first place and therefore had been glad when she had left.

Fortunately to Jayne's mind at least, it was the Housekeeper who noted their arrival and with Luc nowhere in sight Jayne breathed a sigh of relief for she believed that perhaps the man was out and that they could therefore conclude their business and get away before he returned.

"Oh so you're back!" The expression on Mrs Bentham's face was enough to make Jayne wonder if she had been correct in her previous assimilation. "I must say that was a fine way for you to act, leaving in that manner without even the consolation of a farewell! I guess that really upset the master!" Jayne briefly wondered what had changed to have created a bond between Luc and his housekeeper for now the woman appeared to be acting as his protector. "And who have we got here?" Now the woman's eyes had focussed themselves on Robert almost as if Jayne had picked up this individual somewhere in the street.

"This is my brother Robert. He happens to be on leave from the army and therefore I guess he wanted his motorbike!" At the time Jayne was already searching for words for Robert was looking at her quizzically almost as if he had now already guessed by their reception here that she had not phoned the place after all to forewarn them of their coming.

"Oh he is your brother!" Somehow it appeared her words had satisfied the woman for a brief moment before she lapsed once again by allowing her tongue to wander. "Motorbikes, they're nasty noisy things if you ask my opinion. But you came here on one if my memory serves me right therefore how is your brother supposed to take the other one back with him? Surely he's not that accomplished that he can ride two at once!"

"No I came down riding pillion so that I can take the one we came on back whilst Robert takes the other!"

"So you've got it all worked out have you? In retrospect I suppose that is what could be expected of you. But I don't suppose you thought to inform the master of your plans?"

"No I guess we came on the spur of the moment and therefore I didn't get the opportunity!" She was conscious now of Robert's eyes on her as she had now virtually admitted to not phoning up before they left.

"Well a phone call wouldn't have taken all that long and one could consider that under the circumstances such a call would have been in keeping with good manners!" The woman persisted in her attack. "Although I must say that I'm surprised you came here on your own and left that posh boyfriend of yours back home. From what your Ma had to say he is the next best thing to your protector!" Her words now made Jayne take note for if they knew about Simon and the fact that he had come here for her earlier then they must have got this information from her mother and yet she knew nothing of any such call. "Anyway I suppose instead of standing there and behaving as if you have every intention of making a quick get- away you had better come in"

Once Mrs Bentham was in this frame of mind there could be little argument against doing what she asked. Indeed the woman now stood like some retainer of old in the doorway and beckoned them inside. To Robert this was obviously no problem. In fact he seemed to have become engrossed with the building and almost appeared eager to see more of it. It was Jayne who was the one to hold back as she wished with all of her heart that they had managed to retrieve Robert's bike without being noticed and then got away from this place as quickly as possible.

Perhaps her fears were soon to be realised even without Mrs Bentham going to inform the master, for Luc upon hearing the noise of their arrival from his study had himself emerged to investigate.

"She's brought her brother with her, says he wants his bike!" It was Mrs Bentham who offered the explanation accompanied with her usual sniff and Jayne found herself facing a pair of penetrating blue eyes that bulged from under the forehead of Luc Mathieu.

"You never told us when you left!" His voice sounded reproving as if indeed this was the one thing that was predominant in his mind. "Was that too much to expect from you?"

"I'm afraid that I left in rather of a hurry and not of my own volition either!" Jayne found her voice and was now determined he would know the truth for quite suddenly the truth seemed to be important to her. In return he fixed his eyes on her once more as if he was waiting for her to continue. "If you want someone to blame for my speedy exit then perhaps you need look no further than your own father. Fortunately I was rescued from that mad man's grasp by a friend who had also come to see me and who thereupon decided that perhaps I would be far better off at home than staying here to be manhandled by some crazy man!" Now it was her brother's turn to look at her in a puzzled manner for at the time he was still in ignorance of what had passed previously.

"You have met my father ----here?" The recent words that had been spoken by the Inspector now resounded in Luc's ear as he motioned them to sit down. "Then you have no idea where he went to?" The thoughts which now pounded Luc's mind were quite indescribable. Why was it that this girl had managed to meet his supposed father whilst he himself had not the slightest idea what this man looked like?

"At the time all I can say is that I was only too pleased to see that the man, whoever he was, had been dispatched. And I can assure you that I didn't stop to ask him where he was going either!" Jayne began to feel her temper beginning to flare up. What was all this, were folk more concerned about the perpetrator than they were about those he had used for victims?

"Then why did you not tell me all this when I rang up your place?"

"If I said that I was unaware that you had rung up would that level matters out?"

"I guess I can vouch for Jayne in that!" It was Robert now who was attempting to come to her assistance. "Mother often presumes that we need protecting when the reverse is often true. But I guess Jayne was fortunate in one sense that Simon just happened to be around at the time proving perhaps that person does have his uses. Not many I can assure you, I can't say that I am over enamoured by the man myself, but nevertheless in this case one has to admit he was in the right place at the right time!"

"So nobody told you?" Ignoring Robert's rhetoric over Simon, Luc now had his eyes firmly fixed on the girl.

"I'm afraid that this is the first time I have heard of this!" Jayne now felt herself forced to respond although with her mouth now feeling so parched she was surprised that the words managed to come out at all. Perhaps it was as he looked from one to the other that Robert's own remarks were motivated.

"Hey what of it, perhaps the old girl forgot, although even I have to admit she can be stubborn at times when things don't suit her even if she is my Mum. Am I missing out on something by the way, looking at the two of you?"

"We came for the bike!" Jayne now had the expressed desire to get out of this room before she gave herself away. For starters she did not want Robert asking anymore about the relationship she and Luc had forged.

"So I take it that this is a fleeting visit only? But then of course Mrs Bentham will be most upset if her hospitality is turned down in such a manner. Therefore I expect you will be staying for lunch?"

Robert for one decided that such hospitality was not such a bad idea, for this surely would give him an opportunity to look around the house; plus in addition the housekeeper now appeared to be waiting for her instructions and to have declined such hospitality would no doubt have brought the wrath of the gods down upon them. "Brilliant and many thanks although I guess I had better check up on the bike first and see if it is roadworthy. In other words I perhaps need to see that my sister didn't wreck it up on the way down here! I don't suppose you would believe me if I said that I actually took strong objection to her using the bike at all?"

"In that case I will come with you and leave your sister to entertain Mrs Bentham. At one time the two of them got on fine. But how did you get here if your bike was still at this place?"

"Oh we hired another bike. I guess Jayne was reluctant to come until I managed the art of persuasion but in fact I needed her, first of all to find your place without me going wandering off around the countryside, and secondly I actually needed her to drive the hire bike back for me!" Robert was quite non plus in his response but then by this time he had already decided that he had found another bike enthusiast in Luc and when two such people meet then they obviously can find much to talk about.

⋆ ⋆ ⋆

The two men had obviously found a great deal to talk about for when they returned to the Hall on Mrs Bentham's summons, which was something that no one dare ignore, such conversation between them was still issuing forth in full flow.

"Guess what Sis Luc has told me that he has apparently inherited some land in our region and naturally enough would like to cast his eye on it, therefore I have suggested that he comes back with us!"

"But how can he?" The news had sent Jayne's thoughts reeling more especially because this obviously meant that she would see more of Luc and she was determined not to give her emotions on the matter away.

"Simple, Luc likes his motorbikes therefore he can ride back pillion with me for you yourself will have charge of the bike we hired!"

"But I thought that you were not supposed to leave the county area?" She tried to convince herself that she did not know why she now searched to find obstacles to place in Luc's path when in truth it was because she did not want this man to invade her privacy.

"You were right. Actually I was so confined until quite recently when such restrictions were removed!"

"Then the police have discovered who was responsible for the drugs being brought into the country?"

"They obviously know who brought them in for it was the Captain of the fishing vessel. But the person they would like to apprehend is the one who was really responsible!"

"And you do not know as yet who that person was?"

"I have my own ideas on that. But I believe your brother is in a hurry to get going!"

"If you don't mind you will eat your meal before you think of going anywhere!" Mrs Bentham hearing something of the conversation and not willing to provide a meal that nobody wanted to eat now decided to chip in!

"Now would we dare do anything else Mrs B?" It was Luc who now turned his flattery onto the Housekeeper having got to know the woman's limitations and Jayne could see from her attitude that the man had obviously spent his time captivating her.

"And if you go off on this so-called jaunt, not that I totally agree with motorbike riding, how long do you purpose to be away for then?"

"Not long I assure you. It's just that Robert here has now provided me with the means to undertake two matters which I have in mind. First of all I have a yen to see this land which I am supposed to inherit once the will is proven and secondly and by no means the least I have also been offered the opportunity to enjoy myself on the back of a motorbike again. Now you wouldn't really want to deprive me from doing such things now would you Mrs Bentham?"

"That as you well know is not within my power. Not that I fancy the police coming round in your absence and me being expected to concoct some tale to cover for you!"

"Then if they do come round whilst I am away tell them I have gone off joy riding. They are under the impression that the French are mad after all!"

Mrs Bentham sniffed but the matter was obviously settled and therefore Luc and Robert once more had their heads together to the exclusion of all else!

* * *

This appeared to be how the situation remained during the journey back to the North of the country. It was only when they made a stop on route that the topic of their conversation made Jayne feel a little uneasy.

"Well if as you say this land you are on about is so close to our own abode then why don't you come home with us. You can always kip in with me!" Robert as usual was thinking out loud but Jayne was both surprised and not a little relieved when Luc shook his head.

"No, I'll book into a travel lodge locally. If your mother was not for passing on my message to Jayne then I doubt if she would welcome me at your place with open arms!"

"Oh Mum is not all that bad if one discards the weird like notions she gets into her head at times, like because Simon happens to be a banker he therefore must be a good catch for Jayne!"

The girl in question started. The last thing she wanted to hear at that time was Simon's name. There never could be anything between them no matter how much it was desired by others. No doubt Luc saw her squirm but gave a broad smile in Robert's direction.

"Under the circumstances I think perhaps it would be better all-round if I stayed away from your place. That's not to say that you couldn't be a great help in helping me to find this place I am fast becoming fascinated with!"

"Not such a bad idea considering I am a little bit at a loose end at the moment. The thought of leave from the army is great until one has to think of something to do to fill in one's time. Anyway if you book yourself into one of these travel places I will drop you off when we get there and then I will know where to pick you up. Oh and don't worry about Jayne because she can make herself useful by taking the hire bike back before we subject ourselves into paying for another day's hire!"

Thank you very much, fumed Jayne to herself. She would dearly have loved to have exchanged words with Luc but now Robert seemed to be monopolising the situation. Excusable under the circumstances she supposed but then it did little for her ego for she could not help but wonder whether Luc would now want to exchange confidences with her after all that had happened.

And so it came to pass, as Robert had intimated, she was the one who was left to return the bike before making her way back home there to face her mother's tongue once again.

"So what has been going on this time? Don't you think that I was due some explanation before you went careering off with your brother? Goodness only knows what we ever bring children into the world for as they show little respect to the feelings of others!"

"Robert decided that he wanted to collect his bike, something that is quite understandable considering he is on leave. In order to get down to Canterbury he therefore had to hire another bike which he asked me to ride pillion on so that I might bring the hired one back whilst he drove his own!"

"And yet you never said a word about going? Was that because you knew full well I would have most heartily have disapproved? You may have wanted to help your brother, that I can understand, but then it can hardly be considered to be ladylike for you to go careering off around the country on two wheels in that manner. A point I hasten to add that Simon also disapproves of. Talking of that young man he was at a loss to know where you had disappeared to when he came here to call for you for apparently you had made arrangements to go out with him. One might have expected that you would have let him know about the change of heart you had! Really you do not know just how fortunate you are to have that young man dancing on your heels without treating him in this manner!" For a moment as her mother had apparently delivered her speech without taking a breath Jayne felt worried in case the woman succumbed due to lack of air, but then Elaine Taylor was a tough cookie by anyone's standards.

"If I have upset anyone then I am sorry. It was not done intentionally!" Jayne decided that perhaps her best option was to eat humble pie. At the same time however she was loathe to say anything about Luc returning with them for she could just imagine her mother's response if she got hold of that knowledge.

"What land are we talking about anyway? I have heard nothing about any land in the vicinity being passed on to some outsider!" She could almost hear the persistence in her mother's voice if she had spoken the truth about Luc returning with them and therefore Jayne decided that perhaps it was better to keep silent about the matter.

"Anyway as you appear to have returned home where is your brother now if that is not a loaded question?"

"He met up with a friend and they had a lot to talk about!"

"Typically male and then that sex have the effrontery to say that it is the women who talk. In truth I suppose he is keeping out of the way whilst you bear the brunt of my tongue!"

Even so her mother's demeaning attitude did not lift even after her self –confession and with Robert still absent from the fold Jayne decided that once the meal was over she would make her escape for walking along those peaceful country lanes which surrounded Esprick at this time of the day when the evenings were beginning to stay lighter, the daytime still not having yet deserted them echoed a silence of peace when she could turn her mind onto other matters apart from her mother's cries of woe. Yet perhaps even now her regret was not having had the opportunity to have spoken with Luc. Perhaps indeed she had only herself to blame for this situation for she realised that she should have made some deliberate effort to have broken the icicles that had seemingly stood between them. It was an amusing thought but she couldn't help but wonder what her mother would have made out of Luc once she had found out that he owned that Hall for after all she was consistently thrusting

Simon at her merely because he worked at a bank in the city.

Thinking of Simon she suddenly stopped in her tracks. At the time she had been passing the area that had been designated for the future development of the shale gas. The field had been marked out but no further action had been taken in that place as the true owner of the land was still being sought so that he could give his permission for such a venture. Consequently there were no workmen present on the site; something which many of the locals actually welcomed for not all of them had been pleased to learn about such potential development. Now however Jayne's eye was caught by two figures that were currently standing in that field and obviously in earnest conversation. One of these two was completely unknown to her but the other man Jayne recognised only too well for it was Simon Turnbill.

Jayne did not know why she stopped aghast at the sight. O.K. she could argue that Simon was after all a banker and therefore if some client was requesting a loan possibly with something to do with this site in mind this might have warranted some explanation as to their presence. Yet on the other hand she could hardly see Simon choosing to interview a client at night for Simon always adopted the strict code of business matters being conducted only during regular hours which any potential client was forced to abide by, for the banker greatly valued what he considered to be his own personal time away from the office and what was more Simon was a man who abided by ritual.

Something inside of her seemed to demand now that she was not seen, which was probably the reason why Jayne stated to move post haste away from the scene. Perhaps it was this same action that brought her suddenly face to face with two others who had been deep in conversation until her untimely intervention.

"So now what is the rush?" It was Robert who extricated himself from his sister. "Perhaps you are right Luc when you say that women are the most illogical of creatures!"

"Maybe you look as if you have just seen a ghost!" It was Luc who now responded without any of Robert's abrasiveness.

"But what are you doing here?"

"We could ask the same of you?"

"I came out for a walk in order to allow some of the heat to pass from the kitchen back at home. Usually one can find a little peace and tranquillity around here that enables one to seek refreshment from the trials of everyday life!"

"You seem to have a note of desperation in your voice yet by your attitude I guess that today you did not find what you came to seek then?"

"No instead I was to see Simon speaking with some other person on the site which is due for development once the authorities manage to trace the owner!"

"Development, what sort of development?" Luc's features had suddenly become tense.

"Oh Jayne is talking about the new wonder fuel that has supposed to have been discovered which in turn will save us a mint on our fuel bills--------!" Robert paused for a moment whilst he was speaking. "Hey you don't suppose that is it do you –the land you have come to discover for yourself?" For the first time the fact that the land Luc had been speaking of was close to their own home struck home.

"Perhaps we should see who this Simon who is apparently both beloved and yet despaired of by Jayne, is talking to!" There was a determined note in his voice as Luc moved forward in the direction Jayne had come from. Yet a moment later as he reached the bend in the road he stopped as if frozen.

"It appears that your banker friend is actually in conversation with my second cousin!" For a moment Jayne thought that Luc was looking accusingly at her. "Maybe this is the reason why he wanted folk to believe I was a changeling after all!"

"Then this is the site that you wanted to visit?" Robert too seemed to be now viewing the situation through different eyes. Luc nodded.

"It is, I remember the road from the map which I saw. But I still don't understand for even if it is the same land as what he wanted to deprive me of, what has it got to do with the other man?"

"He is a banker remember!" It seemed to be Robert who had picked up the threads whilst Jayne still stood fully mesmerised with what was now going on. "Well, aren't you going to upset their little tete de tete then? You could at least deflate them if you strode across the road now and interrupted their conversation?"

Luc shook his head. "No I guess that I will need further proof of my identity first!" He turned his attention towards the girl. "And maybe you could help me in this Jayne. Perhaps in truth we ought to sort things out between us for I guess I haven't behaved well towards you of late. Now however the reason for my jealousy could have its uses. Whilst I am away could you possibly bear to renew your friendship with Simon Turnbill if only in an attempt to learn more of what is going on?"

"Then you are going back to Canterbury?"

"Of course, I have to for there are matters which I need to sort out. In any case this was only intended to be a fleeting visit so that I could see this portion of land as well as assisting you in returning one of your bikes, or rather having a ride on one for the sheer hell of it! You wouldn't want Mrs Bentham to have some sort of apoplectic fit over my absence, would you? But I promise you that I will be back for I have the distinct feeling that there is something that you and I need to sort out!"

"But how will you get back?" Did she wonder if by saying this she was hoping to delay him, for suddenly the thought of Luc Mathieu leaving seemed to dampen her spirits as if a cup of cold water had been thrown over her and again she fought to find a reason why she should think like this for even earlier that day she had been resenting his presence.

"There is still a form of transport known of as trains. After all it was always muted that I would return that way and now considering I have seen the portion of land mentioned in my grandfather's will I have fulfilled my first intention in coming here. Therefore I will be leaving in the morning after spending the night at the travel inn where I have booked in. Maybe it would have been nice to have been able to spend more of my time here but my return to Canterbury is necessary especially after witnessing what was going on in that field just now. At the risk of repeating myself however I will be coming back for I still believe that you and I have some unfinished business that needs to be cleared up. In the meantime however if you wish to help me perhaps you could find it in your heart to be pleasant to your ex beau and see what you can learn from him!"

Jayne realised it was pointless to argue further with this man once he had made up his mind even if the prospect of Simon Turnbill's company did not exactly fill her with joy. But now the conversation was at an end. She had pointed out some relevant facts to them and now the two men appeared to be ready to leave her.

"Tell Mum I probably won't be in until late. If she wants to know why then say that I have met up with an old army colleague will you?"

She supposed that she had no alternative but to agree as the two men obviously wanted to go off in their own direction leaving Jayne standing alone on the pavement. Looking back at the site she noticed that Simon and his accomplice had also left the scene by this time and therefore there was little else she could do but return home herself and brood over what had happened. For the fact that the land Luc claimed he had inherited was so close to her own homestead seemed to be more than a coincidence!

"So you say that you saw your brother and he claims that he won't be back until late? Really I don't know what the world is coming to for folk seemed to have forgotten all that they have ever learnt about manners. If Robert has met a friend then why on earth could he not have brought him home with him? Anybody would think that we were savages in this part of the world ready to gobble up any newcomer to the place!" Obviously her mother was not at all pleased when Jayne returned home to repeat her charge. At the time however Jayne said nothing to defend her brother for perhaps she was beginning to think that her mother could have a point. "Anyway I still have not heard your own story properly yet. How come you were stopped from coming back home until this stage when you went careering off on that bike?"

"I thought that I told you Mum. Initially I was employed as a courier to take delivery of a parcel from the docks at Dover and transport this to the name that this parcel was addressed to!"

"And could you not have found yourself a more ladylike profession than that? I know that you had been made redundant but a job that involves riding a motorbike dressed in full leathers can hardly be considered to be ladylike. Surely you could have found yourself something a little more suited to you?"

"Perhaps I was intrigued with the idea of being able to motor around the country in the first place and as a point of fact there were no other jobs available to me at the time Anyway things did not go according to plan. Yes I collected the parcel all right but unfortunately it was one that the police took an interest in and therefore I found the goods were confiscated whilst I myself had to account for my actions!"

Her mother sniffed. Obviously Jayne's account of her activities did little to appease Elaine.

"And after that you found yourself staying at some Manor House, therefore it would appear you were in no hurry to return home?"

"But I thought I had already explained that Mum. I was forbidden by the police to leave the area immediately. Therefore without any money to support myself my alternative was to either stay at Priory Manor or else spend my time in some police cell!"

"You could always have contacted me to send you some money if that was all you were short of instead of making a nuisance of yourself at a place we do not know!"

"And have you flying into some sort of a fit at the thought entertaining the police? At the time I believe I took the right option!"

"Tell me why is it that you young ones have no sense of propriety nowadays? Not that I must concede that your brother appears to be any more disposed to that way of thinking with his antics. He comes home on leave, marches proudly with his regiment through the city centre and then appears to think he can do his own thing. I don't think you would find Simon Turnbill resorting to such actions!"

So that was it! Her mother's sole motivation was to get Simon back into the picture again. This time however Jayne did not object!

Chapter Six

Luc supposed that the journey back to Canterbury by train did at least afford him some time to think! Of course the reason why his second cousin now wanted to lay claim to the land he had inherited was now abundantly clear. Stuart Bardon must at least have got to know about the dossier for the potential of drilling for shale gas at this place which was why he was determined to go to any length to disclaim Luc's inheritance. Of course if his ancestor from the Victorian age had been motivated by the canal era then he was potentially off track in purchasing the land there, but again Luc supposed that the Lancaster Canal was not marked at a great distance on the map and therefore the elder statesman could perhaps be forgiven for getting his topography a little awry especially if no plans had been laid out for the route of that canal at the time of purchase.

Yet for whatever reason their mutual ancestor had chosen this spot he could never have envisaged that a century and more later it was not the canal but shale gas which was now the incentive for one to claim ownership of that land. Even so what the other fellow he had spotted on the site had to do with the matter was up to conjecture although from hearsay this man was supposed to be a banker and now he appeared to be indebted to Jayne to find out some more about these circumstances. Not that he would have willingly have subjected Jayne in this matter if she had not been already acquainted with this individual not withstanding that it had been her brother who had put this very idea into his head.

Still thinking of Jayne associating with that other man did little for Luc's ego for the girl he had deemed initially as a nuisance factor now meant far more to him. This was a relationship which he would dearly have liked to have nurtured and yet all the fates seemed to dictate otherwise. Now he ached to touch her body, to kiss her lips and to feel her body yielding to his own. Why indeed did fate have to be so uncharitable towards them?

Finally arriving in Canterbury Luc did not make immediately for the Manor for his mind appeared full of imponderables but instead in an attempt to clear his mind he decided to spend some time in that city possibly hoping that its ancient spires would lift his thoughts and prompt him into action. He realised that his first task should have been to have got into touch with that solicitor to sort out the matter of his D.N.A sample and the reason why the man had been motivated into saying that the results were no proof that he was a direct descendant of Edward Bardon, but then of course the solicitor could not be expected to work on a Sunday for on that day the door to his chambers would be well and truly barred and therefore the matter would have to be left until the following day when he hoped that the man of letters would prove to be in a more helpful mood.

Passing by the Cathedral where just souls were approaching for Matins his feet appeared to take him in the direction of St Margaret's Street perhaps better known for its medieval experience of Chaucer's famous tales. Not that Luc was unfamiliar with this place for indeed this had been one of the places he had paid homage to when he had first come to the city, in addition to which it was situation just around the corner from Castle Street where Mr Withers held his court in one of the upstairs blocks! Nevertheless he paused outside of the attraction, perhaps hoping that the faces of the members of the public who had been in attendance would make their exit full of emotion. Of course it was not only the paying public who made their escape into the streets of the city, for the five tales which were portrayed on this site required actors and actresses to fulfil character roles and in turn it was not unusual to see one of these persons seeking a well-earned break outside of the building.

At the time that Luc was there the one seeking a break appeared to be one who was acting the part of one of the two knights in the Knight's tale. Perhaps the reason why this person had discarded his armoury before venturing outside was not difficult to understand for the steel armour must surely have weighed heavy on the man. What really surprised Luc was the identity of this man now stripped of his finery for if he was correct this person was one of the clerks from out of the solicitor's chambers.

"So this is what you get up to in your spare time is it?" Luc adopted a friendly air towards the young man even if it was a little tormenting in nature.

The one in question grinned for he well knew Luc from their previous associations both at the Hall where Withers had brought him possibly to give the effect that as he was large in employees then he was a force to be reckoned with and certainly not one to argue against. Not that his minions could be considered to be unworthy of their charge for after all to start on the lowest rung in a solicitor office one required a good honours degree in law, and also he knew the man from around the town! "Perhaps I needed somewhere to escape to, for in truth the most complex works of the law are certainly still miles beyond me!"

"Guess my curiosity got the better of me. Perhaps it is unusual to find one on the threshold of a career in law spending his time off in this direction. Maybe one could be forgiven for presuming that you would be utilising time away from work studying with an eye on the future!"

"The truth of the matter is that I have always loved acting and therefore this part time work afforded me some opportunity to be able to recharge my batteries. In fact if it hadn't been for my parents pushing, quite rightly I suppose in their efforts to make me get what they considered to be a proper job with prospects as well as utilising my first degree, if the opportunity had come along then I would probably have opted for the stage. But that wasn't to be and therefore I use my free time to allow myself an opportunity to delve into the realms of the theatre in a modest manner. But that is my story, yet whilst we are here there is something else that I feel I need to get off my chest. The blood results you passed onto Mr Withers. Although I am quite sure that the old man knows nothing about it I have a sneaking suspicion that those results were tampered with. In other words I do not believe that the blood test results received by Mr Withers were the result of your own blood being tested!"

"I don't understand. In fact there is quite a lot about this wretched affair that I fail to understand. Who would want to do such a thing anyway?"

"The ones who seek to gain advantage over you!"

"Then if you know or you have seen anything surely the person you should have reported this matter to was your boss. After all as well as being your chief employer he does have quite a place to play in the entire matter!"

"I don't think for one moment Mr Withers would have believed my story especially when it involved some of his closest friends. As you were a non entity before you came to this place the whole episode was easy to arrange and then carry on as normal!"

"So you are saying that your employer was a party to this deception?"

"Most definitely not: Mr Withers can be found lacking in several fields, but deception is not something that he would condone lightly!"

"All of which then begs the question who do you think is guilty of such deceit?"

If Luc had not been tied up in trying to probe the man's mind in order to achieve an answer to this conundrum, then he would not have failed to see the almost haunted expression appear in the young man's eyes.

"Perhaps it is not for me to say Sir. After all my answer would be pure supposition on my part!"

"And your supposition is then Karl?" The young articled solicitor found a pair of eyes now on him as if they were determined to rake his thoughts from out of him.

"I guess it is time for me to make my way back to the theatre for I guess I will shortly be needed on stage once again!" He attempted to move, to take his leave but by this time Luc had stationed his body between Karl and the entrance to the theatre.

"Once you have told me what I want to know! I accept your answer maybe supposition on your part but at least it will provide me with a starting point in my quest! You mentioned one of Mr Withers' friends?"

"I was thinking of your own cousin Stuart Bardon. His friendship with Mr Withers goes back some considerable time. Maybe it is wrong of me to indict the man apart from the fact that he did have the opportunity and as he happened to be a friend Mr Withers would have no reason to question what he said!"

"Thank you Karl. Perhaps you have just confirmed my own suspicions!" Luc stood to one side in order to let the man pass.

"But what I have told you will remain a secret?"

"I promise you that you can rest assured that your name will not be mentioned!" Luc made the promise not knowing at the time whether he would be in any position to honour it or not. He watched as the young man went back into the building and hoped with all of his heart that it was a promise he would be able to keep!

⋆ ⋆ ⋆

Mr Withers was conspicuous by his absence the following morning when the office opened and Luc swore at having to make yet another journey into town from Barham, the location of the manor on the outskirts of the city, which proved to be of little use.

"I'm afraid that he was called away urgently on business!" The receptionist eyed Luc as if she considered that it was not his place to be here at all. "Did you have an appointment?" The final phrase was added as the woman deigned to peer at him through a pair of horned rimmed spectacles as if suggesting that if he did not have an appointment then he had no right to be here on the premises at all, which of course she knew full well that he had not, for she already had the appointment book in front of her.

"No but I was sure that Mr Withers would have seen me for it is a matter of clearing up the business on my estate!"

"Well as the man is obviously not here he therefore cannot see you for whatever reason you may give. With this in mind would you therefore like to make an appointment? I could fit you in for Thursday afternoon?"

Luc nodded in frustration although in his mind he now realised that Thursday would give him time to return to the hospital for another blood test to establish his D.N.A and then return with it to these offices and demand Mr Withers to compare the results with the earlier one he was supposed to have in his possession. Luc had known his mother well, the two of them had been very close and if there had been any truth in the rumour that he was not her natural child then she would have told him the truth, for such a thing would not have interfered with the bond they had between them. In addition he also remembered what Karl had said about the blood results being switched.

Going back to the hospital for such a test however proved to be no easy matter for the people at that place eyed him with not a little incredulity.

"But the results of such a blood test have already been forwarded to your solicitor, a Mr Withers I believe!"

"I'm afraid to admit it but the man has misplaced the results!" Well this was obviously the truth, thought Luc, for if the results had been switched then the solicitor must have misplaced the originals.

"In that case we should have a record of them here!" The receptionist began to fumble about with a wedge of papers.

"Perhaps it would prove to be easier if I had another D.N.A. test. I am of course willing to pay for it!"

The mention of payment certainly appeared to sway the other's mind. "In that case perhaps you will wait in the waiting room Mr Mathieu and I will see what I can do!"

"Certainly: By the way I believe that you also have a record of the D.N.A of Edward Bardon now deceased. I would be grateful when I receive my own results if you could specify whether you consider me to be a blood relative!"

The idea of receiving payment for this was obviously still very much in the woman's mind. "Ah I presume it is about the estate then Mr Mathieu? Very well I will see what I can do!"

She left him then with a smile on her face and Luc wondered whether it was the promise of payment that brought a more cheerful attitude onto the faces of these people!

* * *

Left to her own devices Jayne was quick to realise that she would now have to be the one to mosey herself back into Simon's favour if she wanted to carry out the mission that had been left to her by Luc. In all truth the only person Jayne felt inclined to make up to was Luc himself but nevertheless as it was Luc who had entrusted her with this task then it was certainly something that she had to accomplish.

Perhaps however her best chance came when she went up into town for some minor detail and actually met Simon in Market Street. At the time he was obviously the last person she had thought to encounter for as it was a week day she had imagined that he would have commuted up into the city. His greeting nevertheless served to surprise her even more.

"Jayne, you are the very person I was hoping that I would run into!" Jayne shook her head passively. Why he had said that upon greeting her she had no idea for after all she had acted on a spur of the moment decision to come up into town herself.

"Why?" She had to be talkative and behave in a manner that signified she was pleased to see him.

"A Gilbert and Sullivan production is on at the Grand this week!"

"Are they?" For a moment his response had flummoxed her.

"Look I know full well that you expressed a desire to see such a performance if ever they came to this town. The fact is that I have also managed to acquire two tickets and that believe me was no easy matter!" At least he seemed to have forgotten all about that previous occasion when she had let him down.

"That's true although I do have my favourites. Anyway why do you happen to be here at this time? Surely you should be at your work!"

"Sweet Jayne always considering where I should be at any given time. But if it pleases you I happen to have the day off today, unusual I accept but the boss wanted something seeing to in this area and having completed that task the time is now my own!"

"So which day did you get the tickets for?" Quite frankly Jayne found it difficult to believe a word the man said but nevertheless she was committed to carrying out her charge.

"Wednesday as a matter of fact: I will pick you up early if you like and we could share a meal together first: Always providing of course that you don't take it into your head to run off somewhere at the last minute!" So he had remembered and he was reminding her of the fact.

"Wednesday will be perfect!" She deemed to pass him a smile; well she supposed that Luc would have expected that much off her. "Which one of the operettas is it by the way?"

"I think it is the Yeoman of the Guards. Oh I know you would have preferred Pinafore but they are not performing that this time around!" Was this man really trying to remind her that he remembered her likes and dislikes?

"Maybe I would but on this occasion that will be fine!"

"So if I pick you up at your place around four o'clock, will that be all right?"

"All right as far as I am concerned, but what about your work: Surely you won't be back for that time?"

"I think that matter can be arranged to fit in with my plans!" Simon speaking of his plans however made Jayne think about the other matter.

"Satisfy my curiosity if you can Simon and tell me what the forthcoming shale gas plant has to do with you work?"

If Simon had not spotted her there he was still quick with his answer. "You forget Jayne, I am in banking and such a project requires funds. I visited the place on the request of my boss the day when I expect you were peering out of your front window!" With this she supposed that at least she could presume he had not spotted Luc at the time.

"As a matter of fact it was my brother who saw you!" She tried to keep herself out of the matter.

"Then he should have come and joined us. I was actually there with Stuart Bardon. Jayne I know that you have had it rough lately with you taking that stupid job as a courier; but please do not pay too much attention to what Luc Mathieu must have told you for even his own father believes that he is something of a usurper!"

"That is something I would prefer to make my own mind up on. After all both Luc and his Housekeeper were kind to me when I needed help!"

"It is easy to entertain in property that is not legally your own. But enough of such people at the moment; I will pick you up as we arranged!"

For some reason known only to himself Simon now wanted to be off, not that Jayne was sorry to see him go but their conversation had still left her wondering how much he was embroiled with Stuart Bardon and his attempts to prove his rights to the estate.

Jayne phoned up Luc that night for she wanted to keep him abreast with the situation and what was more she also wanted to hear his voice.

"Guess old Withers was absent without leave today anyway I did finally persuade the hospital authorities that I needed another blood test!" The way Luc answered her no one would have guessed that they had shared differences between them. "Anyway you are not ringing about that I guess so what have you to tell me?"

"I managed to run into Simon Turnbill in town this afternoon quite accidentally of course for one would have presumed that he would have been at work at that time. Anyway as a result I have promised to go out with him on Wednesday night, strictly in an effort to glean more information out of him!" She had heard Luc groan when she had mentioned going out with Simon but under the circumstances he could not argue.

"Then please promise me that you will be careful. I don't think I trust that man!"

"Funny but that was the same thing he said about you. Indeed he said that you were not to be trusted and that your own father considers you to be something of a usurper!"

"In that case I wonder how the man knows my father?"

"That he didn't say unless his knowledge has come from Stuart Bardon. Apparently the man has been in touch with his bank and that was what Simon was doing at the shale gas site for he appears to be able to take time off his work at will nowadays!"

"Maybe I should thank you for the information Jayne but now I am feeling worried for you! Maybe I should not have asked you to undertake such a project without some support!"

"I have always got Robert here if I need any support Luc and besides you know I will do anything I can to help!"

"Then I must repeat what I said. Do be careful Jayne for I deem none of that shower to be trustworthy!"

Even so and despite the reservations he had placed on her arrangements Jayne never expected Luc to contact her brother with his concerns, but some time later Robert did approach her possibly feeling a little annoyed that Luc's phone call had disturbed him from servicing his bike, which he deemed was now none the better for Jayne having ridden it!

"So what's all this about you arranging a tete de tete with Simon Turnbill?" This was something Robert obviously disapproved of and coupled with the fact that it had removed him from his course of action just when he was becoming enthralled with the inner workings of his motor bike, resulted in him portraying one long face at the prospects of having to babysit his sister.

"There is really nothing to worry yourself about. I have merely arranged to go to the theatre with Simon, my motive being to see what I can glean from sharing his company that could be advantageous to Luc's cause!"

"So I take it that you phoned the man up to make him madly jealous or something?"

"Nonsense in my way I was simply doing Luc a favour for if you remember he did ask us to look out for any detail!"

"And that hardly included ingratiating yourself with the enemy!"

"Robert I have done no such thing. You forget I did go out with Simon Turnbill some time ago, a factor which provided the excuse for me to agree to go on this theatre trip with him, especially as it concerns something that I happen to be interested in. Maybe instead of acting like two overgrown schoolboys you should have applauded this action for this way I can possibly glean some more relevant information for the pair of you!"

"Afraid that Luc does not see it in the same light. Say what is going on between you two? I gathered on your meeting with him that you weren't exactly strangers and now the Frenchman has practically enrolled me into becoming your bodyguard. All this when I have things of my own to see to, such as repairing that bike you managed to wreck. Personally I don't want to get involved with all this Nitti gritty, I had quite enough of it to put up with in the Army!"

"Then you are quite at liberty to pursue your own agenda. After all I wouldn't imagine going to the theatre with someone I have known for ages would constitute a National incident!"

"Maybe not but I still made my promise to Luc. Actually despite everything I think he is quite a nice guy, so please don't involve him in a shotgun wedding. Promise me that you will be careful as you go Sis and let's avoid National incidents and as far as my promise to Luc well you can be sure that I will be close at hand in case I am needed!"

Most probably the only person who was glad to see Simon Turnbill arrive that Wednesday was her mother but there again in all truth Elaine Taylor had always held a soft spot for Simon. Indeed the woman still thought it quite unforgiveable the way that Jayne had treated the fellow and yet despite all that Simon had come back again. In this sense she considered that her Jayne did not know how fortunate she was for there were not many men who would have given her daughter a second chance after she had previously stood him up especially in the manner she had. Of course this was not the only axe that Elaine Taylor held over her daughter for she had now started to bewail the fact that Jayne had no regular job.

"I am sure that you can get something that is suitable for your qualifications. I know it was no fault of yours that you became redundant from your last firm but taking that job as a courier was hardly in keeping after all. Well that job now also seemed to have fizzled out, not that I can say that I am sorry about that but on the other hand I have not seen you making any effort to replace it yet. Surely you don't expect the job to come to you nowadays, it's time you got yourself mobile and started to look for something that is perhaps a little more suitable!" Even as her mother spoke she had sensed Robert smirking in the background although her brother had not said anything or attempted to come to her rescue at the time

Now however Jayne knew that Robert had given a loud guffaw even before he had opened the door to their visitor and then motioned the man inside with a sweeping gesture.

"It's so nice to see you again Simon!" This of course came from her mother and Jayne at the time only wished that it was her mother who was going out that night with Simon instead of herself, not that fate ever viewed such potentials as favourites.

Simon of course beamed in her mother's direction. If anything there was one thing that Simon loved more than himself and that was flattery and then turning cast his eyes upon Jayne he posed the inevitable question.

"Are you ready then? I must say you are looking extremely chic today!"

Even if Jayne could not actually hear him she was sure Robert was once again guffawing in the background and her only alternative was to remove herself and Simon away quite speedily. Not that the thought of her brother making an appearance on stage at the interval of that performance merely to check that she was all right did much for her ego. But the die had now been cast and there were others who were dependant on her so instead she picked up her wrap and told her mother not to worry if she was late back, a factor the woman seemed to be rather pleased about, before she allowed herself to take Simon's arm as he escorted her out of the house and into his waiting car.

The show itself, she presumed was all right. Indeed she might have enjoyed it a great deal more if Simon had not persistently searched for her hand during the performance, which Jayne found to be significantly similar to a wet lettuce. Whether her mother had mentioned anything to Simon about a job for her Jayne did not know for sure but she strongly suspected that she had when over the meal Simon had approached the subject.

"I know that you are unemployed at the moment Jayne and I might have the perfect job in mind for you!"

"Oh!" She supposed that she had to show an interest although the prospect of Simon Turnbill having anything to do with her life did little to enhance her.

"Yes, actually with the advent of this new project in the area the contractors have requested our bank for the necessary funds to open a business enterprise office in the town here, which will be close enough to the site once it has opened. I know that you are good enough with computers and business management therefore I thought it might be a good idea if you took charge of this office; that way you would be your own boss with no one barking down your ears. Of your ability to do such a thing I have no doubt and of course it will answer the immediate question of you finding some employment close to home!"

"So I suppose my mother has been talking to you?"

"Only because she feels a little concerned over you Jayne for she does not like to see you at a loose end and besides with your mind occupied in the pursuit of a new career you will have less time to ponder on the disasters of the past!"

"Oh!" Jayne said the same word again. In truth she did not want to commit herself with anything remotely to do with Simon Turnbill especially in the light of what Luc had turned up about him.

"Of course I will take you to see the office before you finally commit yourself. But once you have seen it and the work that will be expected of you I am sure that you will come to the decision that I am right!"

So it was true, her mother and Simon had ganged up on her; she could almost visualise Robert laughing at the idea and wondered why boys never had to go through these sorts of problems. Still the matter was left in abeyance with Simon fully expecting to take her to see this place but now he obviously wanted to show his true intentions with a floppy hand grabbing her own.

She pulled away pretending to search for her handkerchief and fortunately the ruse seemed to work, still Jayne was glad when the performance was finally over and reaching for her handkerchief again she gave a hearty blow and then claimed she had a headache and suspected that she was coming down with a cold. At least that way she got Simon to take her home early and then feigned that as her headache was worse she needed to go and lie down.

Luc Mathieu was quite surprised when he got the phone call from Detective Inspector Bennett. "Guess I have some news for you Mr Mathieu, we have managed to trace your mother's ashes. Indeed we now have them here at the station and therefore we wondered if you would collect them the next time you get an opportunity--------Yes I know we suspected that they would have been destroyed but they have turned up in the urn provided by the undertakers with your mother's name upon it. They were found when the fishing vessel was thoroughly searched. Apparently the Captain proved to be a little too suspicious to dispose of them. Therefore they are now yours so that you can carry on with your desire to intern them in your family grave!"

Naturally the Police Inspector was now anxious to get this casket away from the police station this being one item that he considered did not belong there and so Luc was only too pleased to oblige. He was also wise enough to realise that now he would have to employ the relevant people to carry out the next task for after all he could hardly be caught digging up one of the graves himself to bury the casket. Yet he owed that much to his mother's memory for now he felt quite sure, after what had happened, that he could not rest himself until he had carried out his mother's last wishes and he wondered whether it had been the death of her father that had spurred her on to make this bequest.

Perhaps it was something of a relief to see that the casket had not suffered any damage after its unfortunate journey but this relief did not extend as far as the undertaker in this country whom Luc attempted to employ to carry out this task.

"I'm sorry but at the moment I believe that the ownership of the manor as well as its lands has not yet been legally settled and therefore it is impossible for me to organise a service of committal or execute the opening of a grave until this position is quite clear!" The man had shaken his head for being a local man he was well aware of the discrepancy of the ownership at that time.

Luc sighed although inwardly his teeth were gritted. Surely even Stuart Bardon could not be so unyielding as to try to stop an act of humane proportions? Yet something in his mind told him that this act was exactly what Stuart Bardon would do if only through sheer spite. The other glanced at him rather sympathetically. "Perhaps the best thing you can do is to sort out this business as soon as it is possible. In the meantime you would be advised to take the casket home with you. As soon as this matter is settled however and I will be only too pleased to carry out your instructions, until then I am afraid that I must protect my name in this business!"

So that was it, Luc took the casket to return to the car. Why was it that he had to find difficulties at every turn? Was his mother never going to be able to find the final resting place which she had specified whilst she had still been alive?

Still there were other matters that were on the agenda now and Luc moved in the direction of the hospital. Now the man was on tenterhooks to get hold of a copy of his latest blood tests and more especially if the hospital kept their promise to inform him whether these could confirm that he was a descendant of Edward Bardon after all. His mind flittered onto Jayne. So far as he not heard any reports of her supposed night out with Simon Turnbill. In truth the whole idea of her spending more time than was necessary with that man sickened his stomach but then Jayne had been in the right position to glean any useful information that happened to be on offer and at least he supposed she did still have her brother to look after her interests. But then that was something which he would far rather have been doing himself.

Whether it was the result of money being mentioned Luc however found the hospital to be most supportive this time around and the information that he sought was waiting there for him. The medic who gave it to him actually had something that resembled a smile on his face when he handed across the paper bearing the results of that test.

"The results definitely prove that there is a genetic link to Edward Bardon you will be pleased to hear Mr Mathieu!"

"At the moment I think I feel more pleased for my mother's sake. I doubt very much that the woman would have rested in peace if she knew that I had been branded as a Changeling!"

"And that I understand is what your own father would have people believe!" In truth this medic could not understand the logic of why any father would wish to undermine his son's claim. "Well I am sure that these papers will prove to the people who are responsible for falsely trying to undermine your inheritance. With this in mind I would guard the papers well if I was you Mr Mathieu. Tell me something though, I know that the Hall and its surrounds are now legally yours, but you strike me as being a man who is in something of a hurry to get this matter cleared up. As an intelligent person no doubt you will know of the long drawn out procedures which the law seem to delight in working through in an almost work to rule manner which in the very least can be said to be long winded, therefore why are you in such a hurry to bring matters to a conclusion?"

"Probably because I need to return my mother's earthly remains to their rightful resting place which is something that the family do not generally approve of!"

"Then if you take my advice Mr Mathieu, when you confront the powers that be with these results I have given you, I would be tempted to take a friend, that is, someone you can trust along with you!"

Luc must have looked a little noncomplex at the other man's words for the latter quickly came back at him. "You do have someone whom you know who is trustworthy Mr Mathieu for I know that you have not been in the country for long!"

Luc's thoughts turned to Robert. The two of them had got on pretty well he thought and he really didn't know too many other people who would have fitted the category. To his mind Jayne would have fitted the role perfectly but Luc refused to involve her wherever she was at the moment. Therefore he wondered whether it was a little peevishness of him to even consider getting her involved. As well as that he was already waiting for her to contact him concerning her dealings with Simon Turnbull. Therefore after due thought it was Robert whom he contacted on his mobile the number of which the other man had willingly supplied when the two of them had been together and had seemingly got on like a house on fire.

"So you are asking me to come down to Canterbury?" The young soldier was obviously surprised at the tenet of the conversation.

"I guess I need you down here. I'm in a position where I require a little bit of support and your name came readily to mind as at least someone I felt I could trust!"

"You make it all sound rather mysterious, but why me?"

"Because as I said I feel that I can trust you quite unlike some of the scarabs around here. I need to be able to prove my legitimacy to the estate. I have the papers but I also need a witness!"

"Then I suspect that you feel Jayne will not do on such a charge?"

"At the moment I would much prefer to leave her name out of it!"

"No doubt she would be most upset if she could hear that. My own suspicions are that the girl is besotted with you!"

"I asked you Robert therefore please can you find it in your heart to help me out in this situation?"

Robert paused for a moment before responding. "Well I suppose I have a week and a half of my leave left if that will suffice. Although I still maintain Jayne will be most upset if she her that she has not been included in this if only for the sake of making her excuses to get away from Simon Turnbill!"

"And if she did then it would only arouse that man's suspicions which we can well do without at the moment. I am not sure how that one fits into this conspiracy at this time but I am not prepared to take any chances!"

"You make the whole thing sound even more intriguing!"

"Then when can I expect you for I am not prepared to take this matter further without a witness?"

"As I happen to be at a loose end how will tomorrow do then?"

"Tomorrow will be fine. We can discuss matters over a meal tomorrow night. Oh just one more thing; please don't mention anything about this to anyone will you?"

"So I am to disappear from this place like a wisp of smoke? That appears to be even more intriguing! Oh don't worry Luc I will see that I am with you by tomorrow night. I'll act as your witness providing that does not entail holding your hand!"

Thus the conversation finished between them and Robert was left to make his own arrangements to travel south again.

Chapter Seven

"But of course you must take the job!" Elaine Taylor drew herself up to her full height even as her daughter still expressed doubts upon the matter. "After all it is very good of Simon to think about you in this way especially after the way you have treated him. What he has now offered to you is a job that is far more respectable than what you could manage to achieve yourself and which is far more in keeping with your strata in society!"

Jayne grimaced. This was typically her mother always seeking to be uplifted in her own strata of society and always depending on her family not to let her down in her efforts. Now the idea of Jayne becoming a central figure in a business consortium perhaps echoed the very lines she would have chosen for herself. "Simon is such a nice young man and really the two of you are so well suited. By the way how was the theatre last night?" This, Jayne presumed, was her mother's way of bringing her back to reality.

"One supposes one could respond by saying that it was satisfactory!"

"You seemed to be back rather early though?" Her mother now wore that familiar critical expression on her face as if suggesting that by returning home early Jayne had not encouraged Simon in any way.

"I saw no reason to stay away for any longer: After all the show was finished!"

Mrs Taylor gulped as she wondered what on earth was wrong with her daughter that the girl had not acted in a more plausible manner. To have deflated the young man so early on in the evening especially after he had found her some suitable employ seemed to have been downright rude on her daughter's part and this was not a matter that one could simply try to brush away. At least she knew that her own mother would have most strongly have disapproved at such an action and she had no reason to question the family adage at this stage.

"Well I consider it to be most foolish of you to have treated the young man in this way. It seems to be apparent from the way he has found you this employ that he thinks something about you and perhaps that is something which you should try to cultivate instead of throwing his kindnesses back in his face!"

"Where is Robert anyway?" Jayne decided to try to change the subject. In truth she had not set sight of her brother since her return from that ill-fated trip when she had decided that however much Simon tried to press his suit, he most certainly was not the one for her and she wondered at whatever it was that she had ever deemed to see in this specimen of manhood.

"He left early on that dratted bike of his claiming he wanted to make the most of any leave he has left. I would have thought that after being in the army he would have grown out of his adolescent fantasies and have managed to get something that was a little more substantial to ride!"

Jayne's spirits sank. After all to her way of thinking Robert was the only bright ray of sunshine around here. She knew of course that eventually his leave would end and that he would have to return to barracks in order to await further orders but that, she had presumed, was something to worry about in the future and at least in the meantime his lively presence had gone some way to alleviate the sense of sheer boredom which she had felt since being home.

* * *

In truth perhaps she did after all allow herself into being cajoled onto taking the job which Simon had put forward. With Robert away and with her mother still breathing down her neck at her lack of aptitude in this field, maybe it seemed to be the easiest way out of the situation and at least she could console herself that it was not in the same location where Simon earned his own monetary wares. Situated as it was in the resort that lay several miles away from Esprick maybe the sea itself with its abundance of ozone gave one the opportunity to be able to breathe more freely. She did toy with the idea of phoning Luc if only to glean his opinion on the matter but then Luc had not attempted to get in touch with her, and neither come to that had her brother and therefore she was left to act independently on the matter.

She was still left musing on the idea after travelling to the resort for instead of making directly to her new employ Jayne decided to spend some time along the sea front there which stretched for absolutely miles, in the hopes that the salty tang of the ocean on her flesh would help to alleviate some of the doubts that still lay within her. But eventually the time came when she felt forced to leave the comfort of the ocean currents and find this new place of employ!

Still the office surrounds that were offered to her were not all that bad and the potential controllers of the fracking episode seemed to be only too pleased to provide her with the furniture and technology that she believed she would require.

"Of course we have not yet received sanction to commence with the drilling, but that is only a matter of time, the powers that be always work at one speed which is often punctuated with coffee breaks!" The man who showed her to the office and handed her the key obviously surmised that she was due some sort of explanation. "But there is still much in the way of preparation that you can do here for we need a degree of publicity and of course anyone who shows any interest in the project will initially be referred to you!" He nodded in her direction quite approvingly taking in her slim figure and the certain personality which appeared to ooze from her pores and which no doubt would, in the long run prove to be good for business.

Still once having supplied her with the earthly goods he thought she might well need in the immediate future, the other took his leave for to his mind he had completed the charge that had taken him away from the site and which he was now anxious to get back to. Not that he fully understood the motive which lay behind this new acquisition, but then he was, after all a mere labourer at this place which was supposed to promote so much attention, more especially once they had received the go ahead to drill and brought the first consignment of this new gas to the surface.

Left alone Jayne looked around the confines of that office. As far as equipment was concerned she could have asked for nothing more but what on earth was she supposed to be doing with it all? Simon was conspicuous by his absence; all right she admitted that the man did have to work on occasions; and her mother after assimilating that her daughter had finally taken her advice, appeared to have acquiesced. At the moment there seemed to be only one thing that she could do, make herself a coffee with the goods provided and then wait to see what happened. The thought of her simply sitting here in wait actually did something to amuse her, at least it helped to remove the tension albeit temporarily for a surprise was shortly due to make itself known.

Indeed she had not time to finish her drink before she heard the office door open and glancing up with some curiosity to see who her first customer would be she suddenly stopped, her mouth now wide open, for the person who had entered the premises was someone she had met before just before she left Priory Manor. What was more Jules Mathieu still wore the same sickly expression on his face as he had when he had tried to abduct her!

"You seem surprised to see me?" He took in her expression with a toothy grin and Jayne could not make up her mind whether this was worse or better than the aggression she had seen when she had come into contact with this creature previously.

"You are not exactly the first person I expected to see coming through that door!" She drew herself up to give him an almost biting response and hoped that this would disguise the chill of fear which now ran along her spine.

"But then things are not always as they seem for that is a fact of life. But there again you could hardly be expected to know that I am in actual fact your current boss!"

"In that case perhaps you will accept my resignation!" Jayne slammed the cup she was still holding down. After the fright this man had given her before she left Priory Manor coupled with the fact that as Luc's father he intended to do that man no favours, this was quite enough to tempt her to walk right out of the place at that very moment.

"I consider that would be most impolite of you considering that you have only just arrived here. Maybe I should explain myself for I am actually employed by the contractors who are currently due to bring the first quota of shale gas to the surface. As they happen to be a French firm then my presence here should not be of any surprise to you. Goodness me you look almost as if you disapprove of such an action but I am afraid that under the circumstances you are expected to approve rather than to allow your mind to settle on other matters"!"

"After what you tried to do to Luc and indeed to myself whilst I was still at Priory Manor, then perhaps your vision is obscured!" Conscious that the man stood between herself and the door Jayne tried to make her voice sound as cutting as possible.

"You of course are speaking of the time when your boyfriend decided to lever a heavy blow to my chin and of course I admire your pluck in mentioning such a matter. But as far as I am concerned I bear no animosity towards the memory of that occasion although in retrospect I do believe that your boyfriend's intentions were to move you to a safer abode!"

"Then Simon knows that you are here?" Jayne swallowed the incredulity she felt rising within her.

"I think not for the man is used to serve our cause only in a monetary sense therefore he has not exactly betrayed you, after all he is a banker and what is more to the point I do not think it is wise to worry him with other details. I also think that you would be wise to abide by that criterion. My main objective in coming here today was simply to advise you on who exactly you are now working for so that you will have no doubt as to whom you owe your loyalty to, and now that I have done so I will leave you to grow accustomed to your new surroundings. One more word before I go however. I think it would be most unwise of you to attempt to inform my son of my current whereabouts. Sometimes I do like to surprise the dear boy in my own way!"

He was gone before Jayne could muster any response even though there were many she could have brought to mind, but now once again she was left alone in that office, this time wondering what either Simon or Luc would make out of this situation.

"So now what are we supposed to do?" Robert watched the expression on Luc's face as he handled the results of the D.N.A. testing along with the other documentation which stated that he was genetically related to Edward Bardon. In truth Robert had expected his new found friend to have been overjoyed upon receiving this confirmation yet Luc held a faraway look in his eyes as if his mind was on something else. "I suppose the first sensible thing is for you to claim rightful access to your mother's burial plot?" It was an idea, for the other man appeared to be searching for anything or at least something and with this Robert hoped that it might bring Luc back to face reality.

"Sorry I was just wondering why we had to go through all this just in order to lay my mother's ashes to rest!" At least Robert could now assume that he had got through to the man. "Maybe the first thing we ought to do is to get these results to Withers!"

"Don't you think that you are being a little too trusting?" Robert wrinkled up his nose for to his mind Luc was far too emotionally involved with this issue to be able to think in a rational manner. "After what has happened perhaps you should consider employing your own solicitor for from what you have previous said maybe this man Withers is not to be totally trusted!"

Luc looked at him for a long moment before speaking, maybe the thought that the solicitor was not beyond reproach had not occurred to him before but now it suddenly struck him that Robert could be right in his thinking. "Perhaps you are right. It just seemed to be natural to go to the family solicitor. I never even considered that his leanings might be rather askew and focussed on the other side of the family even after speaking to one of his juniors the other day. I should have picked up from the tenet of his conversation that things might not be completely kosher at that place!"

"Well I'm afraid that these things do happen in all walks of life!"

"The trouble is I have no experience with solicitors either in this country or in any other country for that matter and therefore it is difficult for me to know where to turn!"

Robert picked up a newspaper that was lying close by and pointed to the name of a national firm. "Guess if you have no one else in mind this firm should do quite well. After all they do have a nationwide reputation to uphold and furthermore they also happen to have offices in Canterbury quite close to the County Courts as a matter of fact if this map in my possession is of any reference!"

Luc nodded as he took in the location indicated by Robert. In all truth he was glad he had this young man by his side for Robert's streak of common sense seemed to be something that he could depend upon and he knew that in Robert he had made a friend.

A phone call was all that was needed to make an appointment which was available to them that same afternoon, much to Mrs Bentham's disgust for this made her two young gentlemen appear to be more secretive than ever as they spoke almost in whispers about it over the dinner table. Moreover Mrs Bentham did not like secrets in this house, especially those in which she was not involved and therefore she resorted once more to her customary sniffs, which in turn were largely ignored by her two young gentlemen much to her disgust. They left directly after eating however and within a short time of leaving Luc found himself outside of the office in Chaucer Road where his new attorney resided.

"You appear to have a clear cut case here!" The young lawyer who greeted them read through the hospital report with a sense of satisfaction probably because to his mind this case did not appear to be fraught with unexpected difficulties and as a young lawyer mainly employed on court issues and often summoned to defend some client on legal aid, such an outside interest appeared almost rewarding. "You are obviously the one who is in direct line for the inheritance and therefore I will have no hesitation in contacting the solicitor who is representing your relatives!"

"And in the meantime whilst you legal boffins sort out all the pros and cons, what am I supposed to do with my mother's remains?" Robert glanced at his new found friend for to this person's ears it sounded strange that in the midst of an inheritance claim all Luc seemed to be concerned about was laying his mother's remains to rest.

"There is nothing to stop you from going ahead with the arrangements. After all you are speaking about a family plot which is involved and no one has tried to deny that your mother was a member of the Bardon family! Please leave matters with me Mr Mathieu for I am sure that everything will be sorted out within the next day or so!" The solicitor stood for the time allotted to this man had obviously expired and Luc left the place still feeling in a bit of a trance.

"Perhaps I shouldn't have left those documents with him like that. After all after what happened before I have little confidence in these people!"

"In actual fact I had them duplicated before we came here!" Robert faced his friend with an expression that made him look older than his twenty five years. "Under the circumstances I thought it expedient for us to retain our own copy especially after what happened the last time around!"

Luc looked at the other in surprise. In some senses it seemed to be good to have a friend here to support him even if this friend now wanted to explore the city whilst they were there. Still he supposed that it was understandable especially as the young man had not been to this place before although he still had to keep his eye on the time, less Mrs Bentham did her fruit cake about them arriving back late!

* * *

Jayne rang Luc that same night. In truth she had been worried that if Jules found out then it would do Luc no favours, yet this was some news which she had to impart to the man more especially as the police had consistently been enquiring whether Luc had seen Jules of late. Yet from being overjoyed on first hearing her voice the tenet in his tones changed when she mentioned Jules and the circumstances in which they had met.

"Look Jayne I do not think you had better go back to that place again! What were you doing there in the first place anyway?"

"I have had a job found for me following on from my mother's persistence. She sort of enrolled Simon into her quest and between them they decided that running a business office in the town would be more of my forte. Not that there is anything to do there at the moment for apparently I am now working for the contractors who hope to commence drilling for the shale gas anytime. Even so I certainly did not expect your father to turn up on my first morning there!"

"You do realise of course that I will have to inform the police of the man's whereabouts even if he is my father? That is why Jayne I do not think you should go back to that place!"

"And miss a splendid opportunity to try to find out what is going on? After all if this fracking idea is supposed to be taking place on your land then perhaps you ought to know something about it. In which case I will continue to sit in that office like the Vicar of Bray, much to my mother and Simon's delight as they will presuppose that I have finally seen sense, and report back anything that I find out: At least for a time that is!"

"Look I will put your brother on the line; maybe he will make you see sense!" She heard Luc speak to someone and the next moment it was Robert speaking to her.

"Look Jayne you have not to put yourself in any kind of danger. Now I have Luc here behaving as if you have committed yourself to the death penalty. With this sort of behaviour I could be forgiven for believing that there is something between you two. Well if there is you had both better cool it for the time being until we manage to sort one or two things out. But considering that I can't be in two places at the same time, whilst you are there on your own, and I agree with you that you are probably in the right place to find out what is going on; then you do not put yourself in any risk!"

"I think you know me better than that after living through all our childhood scrapes together!"

"So with that I presume you want me to give Luc your love?"

"That is something brother that does not enter the equation!" Jayne bit her lip as she lied but there was no way that she was going to confess her feelings to her brother. "I will contact you again once I have something to tell you!" She rang off then now unwilling to promote this conversation any further much as she would have loved to have spoken to Luc again. But that was a matter which she refused to share with her brother. Besides by this time her mother was breathing down her neck wanting to know how she had got on that day.

In truth she supposed that it was a legitimate question coming from her mother yet there seemed to be some urgency in Elaine Taylor's voice almost as if she was expecting Jayne to be able to disclose some exciting news.

"I got on very well if one appreciates perfect solitude!" Jayne did not mention the visitation from Jules Mathieu for to her mind this was knowledge that applied only to Luc and she was sure that her mother had not overheard their telephone conversation.

"Well of course you will have to wait until after the contract is finally sealed and then no doubt you will be inundated with callers at that place from those merely interested in acquiring an investment as well as others who will be employed in the project. But Simon said that it would be a splendid opportunity for you to acquaint yourself with the set up there before the furore arises. What is more to the point is that you will also be paid for being there so that is not exactly bad news is it? Anyway Simon said that he would call round later on tonight!" Her mother took note of Jayne's verbal groan at this news. "I really do not know what you have against that young man, for he is so polite and so courteous. You make no effort at all to encourage the man and I am sure that is what he is waiting for! Anyway as a matter of fact he is calling to see me, although he will no doubt be open to any questions you want to put to him concerning the job!"

"Why is he coming to see you?" It was her natural curiosity that overcame the pledge she had made to herself to have as little as possible to do with Simon Turnbill.

"Simon you may remember happens to be a banker and at the moment we have taken his advice on some investment: After all our money is not earning anything in an ordinary account in the bank. Anyway he is coming here to talk us through some matter and of course Simon has our complete trust for he knows all about investments and money matters for that is his trade. In fact your father and I feel very fortunate to be in the position of knowing him!"

Jayne frowned for nothing like this had been mentioned to her before but then she supposed that it was her parent's business and nothing to do with her, although she did wish that Robert had been present so that she could have shared her thoughts with him. Anyway if Simon Turnbill was coming to this place tonight then she for one was going out. He may have found her this job but that was it and she didn't need to be constantly reminded of the fact. It did seem strange however that Jules Mathieu had tuned up at the very place where Simon had found her this job although after their last meeting she couldn't see the two of them seeing eye to eye. Anyway she had passed on the information about that man's presence that day to Luc so now she resolved to try to forget about the matter. Funny though neither of the men had mentioned anything about the blood tests when she had rung them up. Maybe she should leave such matters well alone and concentrate in finding her own feet in this locality!

* * *

In retrospect it could be said that Detective Inspector acted swiftly once Luc related the news of Jules Mathieu's whereabouts. Neither it appeared was this policeman without influence for within a very short space of time it was the local police from the more Northern county who had carried out the arrest of this man on charges of attempting to smuggle drugs into the country and as the man was wanted for questioning in the south of the country this prisoner was soon to find himself being escorted back to the Dover region.

Here Detective Inspector Bennett soon found that the prisoner had a tale to tell. One often hears the tale of a captured man being ready to squeal on all and sundry to shift the onus of blame away from himself and Jules' tale blatantly stated that he had been forced in his attempt to bring the drugs to England by whatever conceivable method he could design in order to pay off a debt which currently hung over him like the sword of Damocles. The fact that Luc was at the time was hoping to transport his mother's ashes to their final resting place had provided an ideal medium for him for with a little interplay he had managed to use this occasion to his own advantage. Moreover if his plan failed, which it ultimately did, then he had no qualms at then implicating his son in the matter for in this manner he could at least please the ones to whom he owed this debt and who were even now demanding it to be repaid!

One could be forgiven if Detective Inspector Bennett's immediate reaction was to lock this man away and throw away the key for in truth this policeman found the thought of anyone dealing in drugs to be despicable and to involve others who were innocent of such charges made such thoughts even stronger. But there was something else now on the Inspector's mind and that was this so called consortium obviously stationed in England who was intended to be the true recipients of such a consignment and this, decided the Inspector demanded even more questions in an effort to solve this mystery. Thus Jules was locked away for the night whilst the Inspector worked out his method of attack for this officer of the law now had a great deal to think about!

⋆ ⋆ ⋆

Her mother seemed to be unusually quiet when Jayne returned home later that evening and after first glancing around the house to ensure that Simon was no longer holding court there, for in her current frame of mind she would probably have turned tail and run if this had been the case; she turned to her Father as if begging an explanation, for this mood was not characteristic of her mother especially when she had just been entertaining Simon whom she viewed prophetically as a future son in law.

"What has happened?" Jayne managed to confront the man by practically pinning him against the dining table. "Please don't tell me that my mother is not upset over something!"

"I would say that she is fuller of her thoughts than usual and perhaps she is now worrying a little as to whether we have done the right thing rather than simply being upset!" Jayne noted that her father also held a catch in his voice as he spoke almost indeed as if although he knew Jayne merited some reply to her question he would rather have been left alone.

"What exactly do you mean when you say the right thing?" Jayne was still unwilling to let go for these were her parents and although they did not always see eye to eye with her she did not like to see either of them upset.

"It's just the question of the investment we have made!" It was her mother who now responded even though Jayne could see that the woman was close to tears.

"You say investment?" Jayne gently probed further. It was difficult to express the cold hand which now appeared to clutch at her heart.

"I guess we were talked into taking our savings out of the bank and placing them in a capital investment which ought to earn us more interest. It sounded a good idea at the time with interest rates being so low but now I am not so sure!"

Jayne squeezed her knuckles hard. For as long as she could remember her mother had always been shrewd when it came to capital arguing that one couldn't take a brick out of the wall and eat it if one was hungry and therefore people needed assets that they could put their fingers on at a moment's notice. But then Simon had been round that night whilst she had been out for she remembered her mother speaking about some business proposition he had for them. "O.K. then what has Simon talked you into?"

"Basically he was on about investing our money into this fracking business! Simon said that he believed that once the contract was given to this French firm then it would be a very good investment which would be well sought after. And well Simon is a banker after all so he should know!"

"You trusted him and now you are not too sure that you did the right thing?" At least she supposed she had the satisfaction of seeing her mother curl up even further, although in all truth this was not what Jayne really desired to see.

"Your mother always has repercussions after such an event. It is a gamble yes but one I consider to be pretty safe!" Her father nodded his head as if it was attached to some machine on the fairground and then considered that he had made a comment others ought to take notice of.

"And I thought that you were long past the age of gambling!" It was all that Jayne could think of to respond. All she wished was that her brother Robert had been present at the time.

"Oh I consider that our funds are pretty well secure!" It was her father's last word on the matter: "After all one can hardly consider Simon to be a muffin head!"

At any other time Jayne might well have been amused with this description of Simon Turnbill but any further conversation on the matter had now reached an abrupt conclusion and Jayne found herself left alone with her mother.

"I'm sure it will be all right. After all Simon as you said is a banker and he obviously knows what he is doing!" The words were meant as a form of consolation to her mother although Jayne wondered even as she uttered them whether she had said the right thing. Still her mother appeared to accept some form of consolation from them for she even offered a half smile now in Jayne's direction. "Anyway no doubt Robert will be able to lend his opinion when he returns!"

"And just when is your brother supposed to be coming back? Really I cannot understand what made him go off like that for after all his leave is short and his parents would have liked to have seen something of him besides watching him parade with his regiment down the street!"

"He is helping a friend out of town at the moment, but don't worry he still has a week left of his leave and I am sure he will be back soon!"

"Do we know this friend then?"

"Mother, Robert is quite old enough to have friends in other parts of the country. He is not exactly a child now you know so I don't suppose you have even met the man!" Jayne felt horrid at having to lie like this to her mother but on the other hand she was not prepared to say anything about Luc at the time.

Still the woman seemed to be satisfied even with a bad grace. In fact Elaine did not even ask any more questions about Simon, which to Jayne's mind was a blessing at the time.

The internment of Ellen Mathieu's remains was a quiet low key affair with only the immediate people concerned present at the time, but nevertheless Robert sensed the look of satisfaction on Luc's face when the short ceremony was over. In truth Robert had still expected some objection to have issued forth from Stuart Bardon, but the man, whether warned in advance that there was nothing he could now do to halt this internment thankfully remained conspicuous with his absence; and as the new solicitor now seemed to have the other matters in hand, Robert decided after the ceremony was over that perhaps it was time for him to return home if only to placate his mother before it was time for him to return to base.

"But if anything untoward happens then let me know and if I am still in this country I will be down here in a flash. Still I think you have got the right man working for you now, no doubt by this time he will have old man Withers squirming!"

"I really don't know how to thank you even though I realise you have to return to placate your parents. I guess I needed a bit of your common sense!"

"Well you don't have to solely depend on me for common sense you know for my sister is a quick learner. Have you any messages for her by the way?"

"Messages?"

"Oh come off it, I am worldly wise enough to know that there is something going on between you two, or at least if I might be allowed to rephrase that, there would be if it was given half a chance!"

"Jayne and I were thrown together by a chain of circumstances. I will not call them unfortunate circumstances but nevertheless it appears she was already spoken for even before we met!"

"If you believe that then you would believe anything. The whole idea of her taking that courier job, as daft as it sounds, was simply to put a distance between herself and Simon Turnbill as well as the folk who kept thrusting him in her direction!"

"There has never been anything like that between Jayne and myself!"

"So is that the reason she becomes all gooey eyed at the mention of your name? You need to sort it out Luc!"

The other looked across at him a little noncomplex. In some ways he admired the other man's forthrightness on issues which this person deemed merely as trivia that could be sorted out easily, yet he doubted the capacity of the other to understand the complexity of the situation between himself and Jayne.

They had met in unfortunate circumstances that was true enough and what was more if such circumstances had not been quite so unfortunate then they would never have got to know each other in the way that they had. That being said however Luc knew that before he had come into Jayne Taylor's life there had been this other man and therefore he refused to allow his feelings to interfere with Jayne's happiness. He knew of course that she had tried to deny Simon Turnbill, but the question was, if he himself had not come into her life would her relationship with Simon Turnbill have prospered? Perhaps because Luc had these thoughts was why he resented Robert's comments for the boy was after all young enough never to have experienced any of the hardship of reality! Therefore he decided that perhaps he would be wise enough to say nothing.

This of course was exactly what he did and thus Robert Taylor returned back home still none too sure about the truth.

Detective Inspector Bennett was in no hurry to part with Jules Mathieu, for even after this man's confession the policeman still believed that there was quite a bit more to the tale he had yet to hear. Moreover being a policeman he also believed that if he was able to unravel more of the mystery surrounding this person then this would only help to enhance his own career. For instance the Inspector had already been told from his North Country associates that Mathieu had claimed that he worked for the company currently involved in the process of fracking.

Fracking of course was not something of which the Inspector could claim familiarity but then this in no way could satisfy his curiosity and there were obviously places where the policeman could get the information he so desired from and in truth it came as no great surprise to the policeman when he learnt that up until the present time no licence had been granted to anyone to commence drilling for this product and that the only work already previously accomplished in this field was merely to ascertain this gas' viability. In addition such experimental moves had not been executed without a certain amount of opposition more especially when it was claimed that the shock waves caused by such drilling had resulted in minor earth tremors.

To add even further fuel to the Inspector's investigation he also discovered that the area supposedly designated for drilling was on land owned by the Bardon family and as the family home of that clan lay within his own area in the Cambridge area, he firmly believed that such suspicions as he had lay within his right to investigate.

Consequently Detective Inspector Bennett wanted to learn a great deal more from Jules Mathieu before he was tempted to part with him.

"Please allow me to establish whether I have got my facts right Mr Mathieu. You have said that you were currently in the North of England because you were employed by a fracking consortium of French origin, a company to whom you also owed money, which was the reason why you attempted to smuggle drugs into the country in order to pay your debts?"

Jules nodded his head. In his present position he did not feel very much like lying over the matter. All he knew was that things seemed to have gone horribly wrong for him. How on earth this devil knew that he had currently been in the North of England at the time of his arrest, he did not know. There was only that bitch from the shop who knew of his former associations with Canterbury. Personally he had never dreamed the bitch had it in her, but if this was the case when he wriggled himself out of this hole then she would have a lot to answer for. "I've already told you that boss man. I had to keep them happy see! And to keep them happy they wanted repayment. Well I couldn't repay them, I was broke and what was more you lot managed to get your hands on my only assets. So I had to go to them cap in hand, I had to work for them for nought in order to pay off my debt, and that is it. Believe it if you want and prove otherwise if you don't!"

Despite being under arrest Jules stared at the Inspector defiantly. Detective Inspector Bennett muted that his look resembled that of a person who still owns the final key to the problem. Yet even as he gave orders for the man to be taken from his sight the Inspector remembered that the Bardon estate was still within his jurisdiction. Furthermore the one who currently lived there was as well as being Jules Mathieu's son was also the one whom the latter had tried to implicate with the delivery of those drugs. Whether Luc Mathieu had knowledge of this fracking consortium and what it represented was definitely something that as a policeman he needed to find out!

Chapter Eight

The chambers occupied by Alistair Dennett in Chaucer Road were not a thousand miles from the more prestigious position of Bertram Withers in Castle Street and therefore after making a telephone call to acquaint the other solicitor that he was about to make that trek, the younger solicitor made his way there by keeping to the confines of what had at one time been known of as the city wall and which for his purposes provided the shortest route for him to take across that city. Of course to name the rooms which he shared with another half dozen or so aspiring solicitors, who usually depended upon the courts for their livelihood, as chambers was rather a misnomer and a half smile came to his face as he crossed the city, for to be chosen to be involved in a case of this magnitude was indeed a most unusual occurrence for the young lawyer. Therefore in his quest he largely ignored the rain which at the time had decided to grace the city with its presence, for his mind was on other matters.

Alistair Dennett was in fact trying to come to terms as to why an eminent professional from that city was apparently seeking to defraud his new client. Of course he had not totally taken the young man's word in what he had said before he himself had taken the liberty of checking up on these facts, and the realisation that these facts indeed proved to be true only served to puzzle him even more.

Upon his arrival at Castle Street he found the more established guardian of the law waiting for him and much to Alistair's relief the man appeared to be on his own, as if he wanted to hear the young man out without the ears of the others from that office being able to assimilate the tenet of the conversation between them, and therefore Alistair had no qualms at coming right to the point of what had brought him across the city. Moreover he also had in his possession the hospital report on the D.N.A. sample taken from Luc along with the matching report that had belonged to Edward Bardon.

Still if Alistair had expected the older man to flinch when he produced this documentation then he was to be disappointed for instead Bertram Withers had no hesitation in producing a second hospital report which to all intents and purposes proved that the two were not related at all.

"Even so do you not consider it to be strange that two D.N.A. samples taken from the same person over a short period of time should prove to be totally different?"

"I am afraid that I can only act on the evidence that I have been given!" Perhaps by this time Bertram Withers was beginning to resent the younger man's presence even though he had felt it to be a common courtesy to receive the younger man.

"You speak of evidence Sir. What then do you consider this to be which I now hold in my hand marked with the hospital's seal of approval?"

For a moment Alistair considered that Withers was now searching for a response. "I am afraid that I can only act through the evidence that has been presented to me!" To Alistair's mind the other seemed to be a little off put with his arrival for the man appeared uneasy in his chair as he made his reply.

"But I believe that my client previously passed a copy of his D.N.A. findings to you?"

Perhaps it was the word client which made Withers think again and this time after searching through a wedge of files he produced a similar piece of paper from the same hospital. "If you are now speaking of Luc Matthieu, this happens to be the copy from the hospital records which he passed to me!" He handed over the paper and Alistair could see at a glance that contents of the two reports bore little resemblance to each other.

"Then I am afraid you have been duped Sir if this is what you insist you received from Luc Matthieu. The two reports bear little resemblance to one another. But tell me has this paper been in your possession since you first received it to the exclusion of anybody else?"

Alistair was convinced that in the stillness of the office one could almost hear the other man's brain beginning to tick in rapid succession almost as if he was speeding his thought process up in order to find some logical conclusion. To deny that this paper had not left his possession since he had first been handed it would obviously throw the seeds of suspicion on himself and Bertram Withers was not in the prestigious position that he had acquired by taking the blame for any misdemeanours

“No ---well rather perhaps I should say only on one occasion when my client Stuart Bardon expressed an interest in it. But the man gave it back after studying the document practically straight away. It certainly did not leave my possession!”

“And did your client during that time have any opportunity to substitute the paper for another?”

“How could that be possible considering that I was in the office all the time he held the paper and in any case why on earth would the man want to substitute the document? It is pointless to argue that Mr Bardon substituted it with the results of his own D.N.A; firstly because he had no prior knowledge as to what he was about to see and secondly even if this had been possible then the whole exercise would have been fruitless considering Mr Bardon has a similar D.N.A. pattern in his own blood if both men claim to have been sired from the same stock!”

“Nevertheless you must admit that there is a discrepancy between the two readings!” Alistair was determined to hold his ground despite Bertram Withers’ reputation as he tweaked his own paper defiantly in front of the other. It would indeed have been difficult to hazard a guess as to how long this impasse would have lasted if it had not been for one young articled clerk who happened to be on the premises at the time.

He had seen Alistair enter the building and no doubt his only excuse for being there was simply curiosity for it was not often that they had the privilege of entertaining another solicitor on the premises and this particular one was a young man just starting out in his career, therefore John Mason had made himself as unobtrusive as possible in the hopes of learning something of the young solicitor's technique. John Mason also happened to be a person who was also still familiar with the truth and therefore now sensing the impasse between the two elder statesmen he decided that perhaps it was time to make his voice heard.

"But Stuart Bardon did have time to substitute the paper you gave him to hold!"

"Nonsense boy, how could he have done that? I was there all the time he held it!" Bertram Withers cast a withering look in his young apprentice's direction.

"You had to answer the telephone!" The report of his actions came as quite a shock to Bertram. "That was when the man substituted the paper for one of his own!"

"Nonsense, how could Stuart Bardon have known anything about this incident beforehand and even if he had then how could he possibly have got his hands on some rogue blood sample results in the time available? In truth this is a very serious accusation you are making and not one befitting my articled clerk! Sometimes Mason I really believe you bring the creativity back with you from that so called charity work you do at the weekend and allow it to sway your judgement!"

"I can assure you Sir that my so called dramatic enterprises do not colour my judgement especially relating to legal matters. And as far as Bardon obtaining results from a false blood sample, it was the results of his wife's D.N.A. that the man substituted in place of the paper you had given him to peruse!"

"Then if this is true why then have you not said anything about it before, or is it the case that I have to question your loyalty to this firm?" Wither's face now looked almost contorted as he demanded a response and now eyed the other as something of a traitor to the cause.

"Perhaps I wanted to check up on the facts for myself first. After all you have always instilled into me that one should always search for the truth before passing judgement. I therefore took the liberty of going to the hospital myself so that I could check up on my facts. It took a little persuasion before they would tell me what I wanted to know but in the end they did reveal that Mrs Stuart Bardon did undergo some D.N.A. testing quite recently. Therefore unless you can provide me with an answer to the contrary I must submit that this appears to be a feasible solution to what actually happened!"

"And where do you consider that your loyalty lies then?"

"It lies with you Mr Withers of course! After all I could hardly be expected to stand by and watch a man of integrity incarcerated within a web of lies simply because the truth had passed him by without recognition now could I!"

For a moment Withers was sorely tempted to issue his marching orders to this young man. But then Bertram had not been in the profession all his life not to realise that if he now persisted in denying the issue then he could very well finish up in court himself, something that would have done little to have enhanced his own career or persuade future clients to grace his doors. That this threat was obviously on the horizon if he did not comply with these new findings gave Bertram Withers much to think about and therefore it was still some time before he conceded defeat on the matter!

"It is as well that we are able to reach some agreement on this matter for I am sure for everybody concerned that this is a far better solution than having to go to court over it!" After finally nodding his head Bertram found the young pretender extending his arm to him. A gentleman's agreement with the other young solicitor although Bertram did not believe that he had finished with his own clerk as yet!

Mrs Bentham sniffed with something like disgust when she spotted the form of yet another male gracing the doorstep at the manor. The young man who had come from the North of England and who had been staying at the Manor had finally gone home claiming that his leave was almost over and he had to satisfy his mother before it was time to return to his regiment and she had not seen very much of the young lord of late, a matter which pleased her for Mrs Bentham took a positive delight in having the place to herself, for that was when she usually had the place to herself! Even so she had to admit that the whole scenario was far better to her eyes than when that other young solicitor from the town had also decided to grace them with a visit. If at the time she had not known differently, then Mrs Bentham might have been persuaded into thinking that the three of them were celebrating and to her eyes the Manor was not the right place for that sort of behaviour. Anyway that young solicitor had finally left and so come to that had their guest which in turn gave the Manor a far more peaceful entity than it had appeared to be previously, which had pleased her.

Today the young master had decided to stay at the Manor and not go wandering off but as he was busy searching through old records he was not really a worry to her. Now however the advent of this new visitor meant only one thing, which in Mrs Bentham's eyes spelt further disruption.

"I came to see Mr Matthieu!" The Inspector did not know why he had to sound so apologetic to this woman even if she did have the capability of casting fear into even a man of the law.

"He is in the study!" The words came out almost as if they had been stuck in her throat. She supposed that if it had not been a man of the law standing there then she would have made some sort of excuse so that she could keep the threads of sanity within the walls of the Manor, but now she motioned the man to pass her as she indicated the direction of the study and hoped with all of her heart that the two of them did not attempt to stray from this location and thus spoil her new found sanctuary.

"Guess your housekeeper was none too pleased to see me!" The Inspector cleared his throat in order to announce his presence and Luc immediately broke off from what he was doing to give the policeman his full attention.

"I am afraid that I have come to inform you that we have arrested your father for attempting to bring drugs into the country!" The Inspector moved to gaze out of the window where the first buds of spring were now attempting to peep their heads above the ground as if they were still not sure whether the winter had actually passed at long last but were equally determined that if this was a fact then their time to make an appearance on the earth was now overdue.

"I thought that I had already made it clear that I acknowledge no father and therefore I wonder why you felt such a journey to be necessary. Yet I must admit that if you have apprehended the man who amongst other things attempted to attack Miss Taylor whilst she was here, then I am glad about this news."

"And yet there is still one other thing we would like to clear with you Mr Matthieu. The prisoner claims that he was forced into the situation of trying to smuggle drugs to repay money that he owed to a French consortium which is currently present in the North of England. Folk he assured me who could get very nasty if their will was challenged. I admit that I became rather interested in this so -called French consortium, who are now apparently working in our country even though your father persisted that they had legitimate business here. Anyway I tried to do a little investigating myself at this point. Imagine therefore my surprise when I discovered that this consortium was at the moment employed to extract the gas product by fracking in a part of the country which I now believe you can call your own!"

At least the Inspector, pausing for breath, was now relieved to notice that Luc was now taking an interest. "You are trying to say that these people have jumped the gun? They are determined to carry out this work regardless of whether a licence has been issued for them to drill?"

"That appears to be a relevant explanation as to their activities at this moment in time. In addition I can hardly see that the owner of this land has given any permission for this to take place. Or am I mistaken Mr Matthieu?"

"Then you are speaking of my land which is situated in that area Inspector Bennett?"

"What else could I be thinking about? What is more to the point have you as the rightful owner of this sought after plot given permission for such a consortium to take over the development of this land?"

"You must know that is quite impossible for me to have done that Inspector considering that I have only recently had it confirmed that such an acreage was legally mine!"

"Of course which is exactly the point I am now making. For our part we would only be too grateful to learn more about this French operation who appear to have assumed charge for after all this was the group to whom Jules Matthieu claimed that he owed money, the reason moreover, if his account bears any resemblance to the truth, why he felt the need to smuggle those drugs into the country, which of course he intended to sell on the open market in the hope that they would consequently provide him with the funds to keep the so-called wolf at bay!"

"And by all this verbiage on your part Inspector can I presume that you are now trying to persuade me to also undertake to journey North?"

"Why not, for by all accounts you already have friends in that area? Surely it is not beyond the realms of possibility that you should want to look them up?"

"Alternatively I could have it in mind to get to grips with the Manor here and the various improvements I want to make of the place; for surely even you must have noticed that the place is more like a Mausoleum to cherish all that has passed before rather than adopting any scheme of modernisation!"

"Forgive me if I am wrong but I have reason to believe that there is a girl involved?"

"Perhaps that is a factor that one might be tempted to ignore considering the young lady in question happens to already have a beau in attendance!" In truth Luc did not know why he had issued those words for from Robert's own admission Jayne would do anything to get away from this Simon who persisted in dancing in attention around her feet at any given opportunity. O.K maybe had had been a little harsh on the girl after Simon had taken her back again up North, but then he did not really consider it would do much for the girl's morale if he himself showed up on the scene. Far better that she should supply him with any information at a distance!

"You surprise me with your assimilation of the situation but on the other hand I do think that your presence in the place might resolve one or two anomalies in what is happening on that portion of land for as far as I am aware no licence has been granted to drill for anything at the moment even though the preliminary probes have already been completed!"

Luc shrugged for there appeared to be no arguing with the Inspector when he was in this sort of mood. Maybe he did wonder why the policeman appeared to be so keen in establishing what was going on in an area which could hardly be considered to be his own patch unless it was because the law had something which they considered to be of more importance on this French firm that was supposedly operating on the site. He remembered too about the offices that had apparently been set up in a nearby resort where Simon had apparently found Jayne a job, and thinking of Jayne Luc suddenly began to worry about the girl. Still he waited until after the Inspector had left before he made his move.

His first contact was with a rather surprised Robert who was at the time familiarising himself with his mother's mood and at the time was only too pleased to be offered a diversion even if this was only for a short time, for after assimilating what was going on in that household Robert decided he needed something to take his mind off things before he had to report back to his regiment. Therefore that task completed Luc booked himself some accommodation before informing Mrs Bentham that he would be away for a few days.

Of course such news left Mrs Bentham shaking her head and proclaiming that she never would understand the young who seemed to be incapable of settling down anywhere for longer than twenty four hours. Of course she blamed all these new electronic methods of communication that existed nowadays for the young seemed to be hell bent on moving around just as fast as their digital impulses travelled, for surely before such contraptions had come along the young had been content with a more stable existence!

"Perhaps you would do better if you thought of settling down back here at the Manor!" It was her way of reprimand. "Anyway I guess this place could do with a woman's touch, someone preferably who is capable of sorting you out. What about that girl who stayed here for a while? I was even beginning to think that the two of you had something going between you!"

"I guess Jayne had matters of her own to sort out. No I will be away because I now feel that it is imperative to take a closer look at this land I also appear to have inherited!"

"Oh that. In all truth I don't know why the master didn't sell it. Simply hanging onto some useless acreage just because it was left to him by his ancestors, was a definite misdemeanour on his part and if you take my advice you will make short shift of the place for after all it is hardly within easy access of the Manor. Maybe you could find a buyer for it whilst you are up in that area because I have heard that these builders are always after acquiring additional plots for future development. That is always providing anyone in their right minds wants to live in that part of the country!"

"I can assure you that contrary to the southern belief ,that north of Watford the folk who happen to live there can hardly be considered as savages!"

"Then have it your own way if you must, go there and endeavour to waste even more time!"

"I can assure you Mrs Bentham that my time there will not be considered as wasted!"

"As I said before, have it your own way then!" The woman sniffed for she was certainly not persuaded by Luc's argument. "Just be good enough to let me know when you plan to return so that I will be able to cater to your needs for when you get back!" Having now exhausted herself by speaking her thoughts the woman decided that she would be better employed elsewhere and therefore she removed herself from the room with the greatest dignity that she could muster passing from the place like a wave that must surely have frightened the Titanic.

To say that Stuart Bardon, upon receiving the news from Withers that Luc Matthieu did have a legitimate claim to the estate, was livid, would be a complete underestimate of that man's true feelings. Under the circumstances it was possibly a mood that one could have expected even if the intensity of this man's emotions could never have been measured. Furthermore at being confronted with such a catastrophic catalyst Stuart Bardon had by nature to look around to apportion the blame.

The immediate person who happened to be the first in line for his scorn was naturally enough his wife whom he now blamed for producing the wrong sort of blood sample after she had been cajoled into donating this in order to discredit Luc Matthieu. If the latter had been anyone else but a relative Stuart Bardon would probably have ignored the details for he was not over enamoured with Frenchmen in the first place. Indeed maybe his emotions on this nationality was more reminiscent of someone living during the years of the hundred years war and even now he failed to realise the legitimacy of fighting the Germans in the twentieth century when surely it should by the merits of history, have been France whom this country had fought. Still he would have expected his wife to have at least produced a blood sample that would have withstood anything that Luc Matthieu could have produced.

All of this of course he took to explaining to Simon Turnbill through the cacophony of grunts and wails which reached the ears of the recipient and which were so frequent that it is doubtful whether the young banker could understand one iota of what he was talking about. Still there was one item that seemed to wriggle its way to the top in order to become audible enough and that was the name of Luc Matthieu; the sound of which caused Simon Turnbill to produce an expression which resembled a sneer on his face. This expression was of course further emphasised when he also learnt that the person bearing that name also had the intention of inflicting himself on their neighbourhood.

"But why on earth does he want to come here if he had got his mansion to sort out down south?" Now it was the sound of condemnation that perpetrated the noise made by Simon Turnbill's lips. Not that he had anything against the man personally apart from the fact that he seemed to be hell bent on breaking up his own cosy relationship; no it was that girl whom he was now considering, for after all he had his own plans as far as Jayne Taylor was concerned. Unfortunately he never seemed to have the opportunity to get close to her nowadays even if she did owe him some thanks for finding her that job. The major obstacle to this factor at the time appeared to be her brother who was currently on leave. Not of course that he would be present in the area for very much longer for Simon believed that he was due to report back to his regiment at any time and that would be a blessing in disguise. He had also another reason for wanting to see the back of Robert Taylor for that young man could become altogether a little too personal and if he perchance should make enquiries into his parents investments and find out whom they had put their trust in, then the young man would at the very least be a little ratchety. Thus Simon Turnbill was not over impressed with the comment that Luc Matthieu was also due to visit these parts for as far as he was concerned then the Southerners should stay in their allotted span.

"I would imagine that his intention is now to cause trouble that is unless he is stopped!" Stuart Bardon invoked the right amount of emphasis to his voice as he carried on with the conversation. "I don't imagine for one moment that you would welcome him acquiring the knowledge of your own part to play in our recent dealings!"

The man had said his piece and in doing so he had successfully achieved the matter he had set out with every intention of completing. For Simon Turnbill was now motivated to cover up his own back, which meant, as far as Stuart Bardon could see that he had further cemented the other man's loyalty, and that to Stuart Bardon's mind was what this game was all about. Even so there was still one other item that Bardon felt he could fan such flames with, aye and possibly help himself at the same time.

"The land close to the airport, the acreage I believe you said was to let; is it still available?"

Simon Turnbill nodded. He had no idea as to what had promoted Bardon's question but he did know that the portion of land he was speaking about was still in the hands of the bank. In more affluent times the land would probably have been sold for prime development but today's economic climate did not bode well for it achieving a goodly price and therefore the bank was attempting to let it on a temporary basis.

"Then if that is the case perhaps you could acquire it for me on a short term let?" Bardon gave a coarse laugh as he watched Simon's expression. This man because he was a banker thought that he knew everything when in all truth he was but a mere novice in the art of manoeuvring.

"You are speaking of the acreage adjacent to Radar Lane?" Simon was still puzzled.

"I am, for once you have acquired this for me then I have no doubt that I can persuade the drilling company to move a few yards further away for another exploratory drilling, which means that when Luc Matthieu come s to claim his own acreage there will be no sign of this company on his land. Of course the move will only be of a temporary nature that is why I only require a short term let, for once the man is dispirited then he must be persuaded to sell his acreage. After that I am sure that the drilling company will be only too pleased to resume their former practice!"

Stuart Bardon held out his hand to the young banker for after all this one could still be of some use to him and Simon Turnbill now believing that the bank would be pleased with him for obtaining a tenant for the land they were holding and might be inclined therefore to forward him some sort of advancement, took the hand and shook it in agreement.

After spending twenty four hours in the family house Robert Taylor was really beginning to wonder why he had bothered coming back, for whilst his father did at least treat him as an adult, his mother still appeared to have the idea that he was still a juvenile and thus as well as listening to her frequent lectures he also found himself frowned upon if he sought to do his own thing. Consequently upon receiving the phone call from Luc that something had come up and he needed to come back to the area, Robert felt the flow of vast relief. He did wonder whether he ought to mention this pending visitation to Jayne for since her experience at that office with Jules Matthieu she appeared to be but a shadow of her former self. Probably what put him off saying anything was the fact that Simon Turnbill had now made a habit of frequenting the place and although Robert knew his mother was still pushing his sister in that direction, he still puzzled as to why Jayne had not stood on her own two feet and told this dedicated beau where he could go.

The Premier Lodge where Luc was staying was almost within walking distance of the family home and it was also a comfortable place where one could relax outside in the grounds. Consequently when Luc did arrive it was to find Robert already there waiting for him.

"Well it didn't take you long to find your way here!" Luc had spotted him as he turned off the motorway junction close by. "Don't tell me that you have already had enough of the homestead already?"

"Something like that!" Robert grinned at him whimsically. "In fact I am in two minds as to whether to check into this place with you!"

"And have the family turn up en block to escort you home? I think not!" Luc forced a grin in his direction even though his mind was still on other matters. "Even so there are other items that have promoted this visit. I mentioned that I have had the Inspector round again. Well apparently I have been advised to check up on one or two anomalies in connection with that land for apparently our friends are acting without license!"

"Not anymore. As a matter of fact they have suddenly up't sticks and moved with their surveillance gear down the road a mile or so!"

"You mean to say that they knew that I was coming?"

"I presume that is quite likely. On the other hand they cannot be apportioned blame for further surveillance even if it all happens to be in the same gas field. The reason that I know about this is that Simon Turnbill let it slip when my mother questioned him as to where they had suddenly moved to and he said that there was nothing unusual about them doing this especially when the whole project is still in its experimental stages!"

"But I understood that they were beginning to drill even without the recognised authority?"

"I would suggest that these people are masters in their craft at being able to cover up their traces when it suits them so to do!"

Luc's expression on Robert's words was sombre as if he was now reflecting upon the matter an attitude which lasted all of two minutes before he snapped his fingers.

"In that case shall we go and see for ourselves?"

The distance from the Premier Lodge to Luc's acreage was not far and therefore the two of them walked along the road which at this time of the day was now thronged with traffic, until they reached the garage behind which the acreage which Luc had inherited lay. The land was in fact easy to access but just as Robert had previously said there was now no sign of anyone from the company in question there and neither was there any equipment left behind after they had left, although one thing did make Luc think that these people must have left in a hurry and recently too for the ground where they had been working had still not recovered from the impressions they had made. After staring at it for several minutes Luc finally turned to Robert.

"And this other site, the one you spoke about close to the airport?"

"Guess we will need transport for that but as I am currently so close to home I can always get my bike!"

Luc nodded for his mind was far too full of other things to pay much attention to what the other man was saying, but a few moments later and he found that he was riding pillion again. Still when they arrived at the new site although the equipment had been set up there seemed to be little evidence of any work being carried out. Indeed the notice that the land was to let had still not been taken down.

"So you are saying that in actual fact the bank still owns this land!" Luc nodded up at the board.

"As far as I am aware that is correct!"

"And I can assume that this is the bank which Simon Turnbill has some interest in?"

"That I believe is correct also although I would imagine that he is still only a very small cog in that organisation!"

"Nevertheless the man is still associated with them and if my memory serves me right it was Simon Turnbill whom we saw talking in that field to Stuart Bardon when we were last here!" It was a voice that was full of thought and Robert could swear he could hear the wheels of reasoning now turning in the man's head.

"I believe you are right about that. The thing is now we have come here are you not going to say something to someone from this consortium that is working here?"

"In all truth there does not seem to be much evidence of any work being carried out at the moment. But there is something else. Now that the drilling appears to have been halted does your sister still happen to be at that office in the town?"

"Why yes I believe she is. In fact I believe that Simon was most insistent about her carrying on there even if there was little to advertise considering the drilling had been halted. Perhaps the man was simply trying to find her work or else he was trying to please Mum and Dad in his own indomitable style!"

Luc chewed on his finger for a moment. "I think that perhaps it is time that I met your Mum and Dad. You can introduce me as your friend if you like!"

"Maybe I would like it better if I knew exactly what you had in mind!"

"And why should there be anything devious in my mind. I merely wish to make their acquaintance and perhaps get a better chance of speaking to Jayne. To be quite frank I am certainly not au fait with the idea of her still working at that outlet especially now when the whole idea appears to be defunct!"

"And that is all that you are worried about concerning Jayne?" Robert posed his words quite slowly and distinctly almost one could have imagined with tongue in cheek.

"If there was do you think I would tell you?" Luc was now determined to give nothing away. "Anyway who knows perhaps you will learn more once you introduce me to your Mum!"

Robert shrugged for he realised there was no point in arguing with the man any further. Now he would just have to wait and see what this person had in mind for Luc Matthieu was determined to give nothing away.

★ ★ ★

Elaine Taylor showed some surprise with the advent of the young man whom Robert brought home with him that day. Of course she was used to Robert bringing home his friends in the past, but this person was decidedly different more especially when Robert announced that the chap came from Canterbury.

"So you must be from the Manor where Jayne stayed a while back?" A puzzled expression now governed Elaine's eyes for up until the present time she had not had a clear answer as to why Jayne was staying there in the first place.

"This is Luc yes!" Robert obviously had no intention of letting the other speak for himself. "Luc actually owes the Manor down there and he also owns some land in this area which is why he is currently paying us a visit for he has come to look it over for himself!" Robert cast a wary eye in Luc's direction intimating that perhaps now was not the best time to inform the woman that Luc actually owned the land that they had been drilling on a short time before.

At least the mention of Luc being a property owner as well as owning some land in the area seemed to lighten Elaine Taylor's features for she now almost smiled in Luc's direction when she subsequently spoke to him.

"Then of course you must have come to see Jayne. I am afraid that she is at work at the moment but I do believe that you are to be thanked for the way you befriended her when she had that spot of trouble. Mind you I could never understand why she ever went off on Robert's motorbike like that. If she had to go down to the South coast one might have expected her to have adopted a more civilised way of travel!" She caught Robert's expression for now he was openly grinning at his mother intimating that travelling by bike was not to be considered civilised. "Oh it might be all right for young men especially teenage boys but one would anticipate that even they would grow out of the habit when they reached maturity!"

"You must have realised by this time that my mother is not over fond of motorbikes!" Robert still seemed to find the interlude amusing.

"You are quite aware of my feelings about them!" Elaine dismissed her son's rendition as pathetic and turned her attention back onto Luc. "We never did get the full story as to what Jayne was actually doing down there Mr Matthieu; maybe you can enlighten us?"

"Jayne was doing nothing wrong. She had merely taken a job as a courier and was doing this to the best of her ability. I don't suppose at the time that she ever dreamed that she would become mixed up with certain elements of my own family tree!"

The woman was dying to hear more by this time but somehow knew that she was hardly likely to obtain it from the man in front of her, not at that particular time anyway. Perhaps therefore it was in this mood of curiosity that she issued her next phrase. "Anyway you must stay for a while Mr Matthieu for I am sure that Jayne will be pleased to see you when she returns from her work!"

Luc sensed that Robert who was by his side at the time, was now practically convulsed with the dialogue for to Robert's mind, Elaine now having discovered that their visitor had inherited a Manor house as well as some land in this very region, would most definitely be waiting to make her kill or at least secure for herself a passage to the land of the upper echelons!

Chapter Nine

In the event they did not have to wait for very long before Jayne arrived home. The only trouble now, as far as the boys were concerned, was that when she actually arrived she was not on her own and Robert was possibly the first to groan when the figure of Simon Turnbill followed her into the house.

"I am sorry. I see that you have visitors!" The expression in this newcomer's voice however did not signify regret but rather a more belligerent note as if he could not come to terms with what the two were doing here. Robert of course lived here and therefore Simon knew that he had to accept his presence at this time, the only saving grace lying in the fact that he was aware that he would be shortly returning to his regiment and therefore his presence could be tolerated. But as for the other one; well Simon Turnbill knew full well where he had come from and what worried him now was why this man had decided to pay them a visit. Unless of course this fellow had come to see Jayne! It was a sneaking thought that suddenly occurred to him but nevertheless it was something that also hit him hard for to his mind he now considered Jayne to be his own private property and furthermore the look in the girl's eye upon espying this creep from the South of the country served to increase his unease. "Jayne and I had planned on going out anyway, she only called home to inform you of the fact, therefore if you have visitors then we will depart quickly for I am sure you will not want us around whilst you are entertaining!"

"Nonsense Simon, Robert's friend only called in to see me so that I would know whom Robert preferred to spend his leave with!" It was Elaine who entered the fray for at the time she could not understand why Simon appeared to be so upset at her guests' presence. "Oh this is Luc by the way. I believe that he has just inherited some rather distinguished property in the Canterbury area. As a matter of fact I was just goading him into telling me all about it! Perhaps you would like to hear all about it too?" It was an invitation given generously on Elaine's part and perhaps fortunately enough she was not able to see the expression which distorted Simon's face when she offered it.

"I have heard about it beforehand and therefore the story of that is not unfamiliar to me. But so that you can hear all the details in peace then Jayne and I will take our leave. As a matter of fact I have promised to take her to see a show tonight!"

Jayne cast him a look of helplessness and Luc clenched his fists. For two pins he felt that he could willingly have landed out at this man, but then considering that he was in somebody else's household at the time this was something that he could not do. There was an efficient click of the heels, which to Luc's mind seemed to be very reminiscent of a certain regime in World War Two and then the intruder who appeared to have come from nowhere took Jayne's arm and practically propelled her out of the place.

"I am afraid that you must excuse Simon. His manners are of course impeccable. The only thing is that he does not like anything that might upset any plans he may possibly have made. Still as he comes from a good background, Simon of course is in banking, I suppose one can say that his mannerisms are really what I consider to be acceptable! Of course this is not the first time that they have been to see a show together; Simon will not drive to the metropolis but there is a very good train service that will take them right into the heart of theatre land in Manchester!" The words were spoken almost as if they were an apology although in all truth Elaine Taylor spoke the words as if she had something very definite to say. In truth she had been more than delighted when Simon Turnbill had shown a preference for her daughter, but now here in front of her was another individual whom she also considered having prospects and now she dearly yearned to learn more about him. "Anyway no doubt the two of you will stay for tea even if my daughter has been whisked away like some blithe spirit?" She turned her wide open eyes on the two boys as if by doing this simple thing she could exert some charm over them and persuade them into her ways.

"Sorry Mum, Luc is staying up at the Premier Inn by the roundabout and we have already booked a meal there for this evening!" It was Robert who was now making an effort to escape perhaps because he already knew of the third degree his mother was likely to put Luc through during the meal if they ventured to stay here.

"But Robert your leave is almost over and we have seen hardly anything of you!" At least Elaine now felt she had reasonable grounds to show a pout on her face.

"I am due to report back the day after tomorrow so I promise that I will give you some of my undivided attention before I return. In the meantime Luc is interested in finding his land in this area!"

"And where exactly is this acreage, do you know?"

"I believe that it lies in the area behind the garage on the road quite close by as a matter of fact!"

"But isn't that the place where they were on about drilling for that funny gas?"

"Yes it is the same place! The only thing is though that now all the so-called drillers have all gone, they appear to have disappeared into thin air as well as taking every last piece of equipment with them!"

"But why have they done that?"

"That of course is what Luc would like to know. Isn't it Luc?"

The other man nodded. In a way he resented Robert tormenting Elaine in this manner even though he knew that Robert was only trying to establish what his mother knew about the matter, if anything. But then Robert had obviously had enough of being in the tormenting mode for the time being for he indicated that perhaps now was the time for them to leave. Therefore they left the place without either Luc being able to speak to Jayne or even establish any answers to the questions which still lay buried inside of him! They left leaving Elaine Taylor still feeling a little miffed for the woman prided herself on the fact that she was well on the way of extracting some new information from this most fortunate of encounter. After all it was not often that one had the good fortune to have a landowner of such merit within the household; and to let the man escape in that manner was not exactly Elaine Taylor's ideal especially when there appeared to be plenty of money on offer!

* * *

Robert was still chortling even after they reached the road outside of the house. "I guess she got you in there mate. Never let it be said that anything that has to do with money easily passes Elaine's eyes. No doubt she will be trying to weigh up which one of you could offer Jayne the most in the way of finances by this time! Speaking of Jayne however I guess I am sorry that you didn't get the opportunity to speak to her!"

"I guess that Simon Turnbill has more than one question to answer!" Luc's lips were tightly drawn. "This office you said that Jayne worked at, is there any chance of us going there?"

"The question is, should I give you directions of how to get there on your own or shall I spend the last day of my leave taking you to the place?"

"I am quite capable of following directions on my own!"

"I am sure that you are but then I think it might be better under the circumstances if I came with you!"

"Why are you expecting trouble or something?"

"Not really, it is just a hunch that I have!" Robert refused to say anymore. Instead his mind had reverted back to the meal that they had booked and consequently he pushed any thoughts of his sister conveniently into the background. Luc however was left with his own thoughts to ponder on as well as the tense feeling he had felt deep inside of him when he had seen Jayne with Simon Turnbill. Perhaps at the time he had never stopped to notice the look in Jayne's own eyes when she had been hustled out of the family home for if he had perhaps he would not have felt quite so dispirited!

Jayne was still having thoughts about the matter of seeing Luc again even as Simon slobbered over her during the evening meal and by that time she was wishing that she had possessed the courage of her convictions and had refused to go out with Simon that night even if such a refusal had been on the last minute. Besides she had other things on her mind at the time for a communication from the court had informed her that she would be required as a witness in the Jules Mathieu case which would shortly be receiving a court hearing. Her mother no doubt would have thrown a fit wondering where all the etiquette and good manners she had instilled into her daughter had disappeared to but to Jayne this no longer seemed to matter, not when she had cherished the thought that she had the opportunity of speaking with Luc. But there again perhaps the man did not want to speak to her for after all he was present in the house as her brother's guest which did not mean that he had come to see her!

It was Simon who was the one to finally break the protracted silence between them as he attempted to take hold of her hand across the table. "Jayne we have known each other for some time now and therefore I am sure you must know what is now on my mind!"

Jayne took a long drink from her glass and tried to ignore him. Of course she knew well enough to what he was now inferring and no doubt he had been prompted in this task by her mother, but in all truth this was not something that she wanted to hear. But still the man hung onto her almost as if he believed that by doing so he would be able to bend her to his wishes and of course Jayne could not keep the glass to her lips for ever more.

"What would you say if I proposed that we should become engaged? After all we have known each other for long enough and I think that you know of my intentions towards you. Perhaps in a way I do not feel that my intentions have proved to be unwarranted and therefore I am sure that your parents would now welcome some sort of official agreement between us!"

"And what if I was to say in response that I am not sure in my own mind?" Simon's attitude made it difficult for her to totally refuse him. In fact she almost believed that by her doing so the man would most definitely blow a fuse or something. But the acquaintance of another had now convinced her that she had no future with Simon. Whether the other person returned her emotions she did not know but feeling the way that she did she certainly could not attach herself to Simon and therefore whatever happened in the future it was far better that they should break up now and forget all about any pending relationship.

"I would say that you are probably confused which is, I suppose, not surprising considering the recent turmoil you have been put through. Not only that but I am sure that the unexpected arrival of that man at your mother's place today has also unnerved you. Personally I think that his appearance here was a confounded cheek and I have a good mind to speak to your brother about it. He may profess to own a mansion, the truth of which can be doubted if what my contacts tell me is to be believed, but quite honestly his lack of breeding leaves something to be desired. After all was it not his father who attacked you in the grounds of that place where fortunately I just happened to be on hand to rescue you. Goodness only knows what would have happened to you if I had not been there!"

Jayne glanced in Simon's direction. By this time the other had become quite puce in the colouration of his face following his verbatim as if this had been made with some tumultuous effort on his part. "Look Simon, Luc has nothing to do with this. I take exception to what you say about his breeding and his rights to own the manor, that is true and I do not deny it, but whether Luc had been around or not there could never have been anything more than friendship between us and such a friendship is something that I have always valued us!"

"Then maybe I can make you change your mind once you have had the time to consider it. After all I am not without status myself. At least allow me to live in hopes that you will change your mind?"

"I am sorry Simon but as much as I know that my mother would like us to make a go of it and no doubt would be over the moon about such a decision, the answer is no. I value your friendship but I do not feel for you in any other way and therefore if you persist with your foolhardy determination I can only visualise that this will damage any vestige of our friendship!"

Jayne had finally reached the end of her rhetoric. In actual fact she had surprised herself with what she had said yet on the other hand she felt that she had to make her position clear whether Simon appreciated it or not. Luc did not enter into the equation for by this time she firmly believed that he saw their relationship existing only as two ships which had been brought together through disastrous circumstances and now that such matters had been resolved Luc obviously preferred to go his own way. What she really felt in her heart did not enter into any equation but she now knew that she would not finish up her life living with Simon and therefore the man had to be told.

To do him justice Simon did manage to portray the art of friendship for the remainder of the evening for if he had not then Jayne was convinced she would have left him on the spot. Yet there was something in the man's eyes that still expressed disbelief at her words almost as if he wanted to challenge them and convince her that she was in the wrong!

* * *

Jayne returned home early that evening to find her brother still up and around the place even though she had surmised that he would have been staying at the lodge with his friend on that particular night. What was more it also appeared that her brother had been waiting for her return.

"I must say that I thought you would have had something decent to say to Luc earlier on. After all the two of you must have got to know each other pretty well whilst you were staying at the Hall!"

"I did not stay there through choice if you remember. Neither did I stay because Luc invited me. No, we were actually thrust together by one policeman who considered us both to be involved in certain criminal activities and who wished to keep us within the area whilst investigations were carried out. Upon hearing Luc's version of events I admit I did feel a certain sense of sympathy for the man but that is all and sharing our troubles was the only thing that we had in common. As I did not expect to see Luc here earlier tonight and I had already promised Simon to spend the evening with him I saw no problem in carrying on with my arrangements as I had previously planned!" Jayne sighed for she could not tell her brother how the sight of Luc had sent her heart racing earlier that night and in any case she had been requested to keep up her friendship with Simon to see if she could unravel some plot which involved the bank and that drilling consortium.

"Oh of course I had almost forgotten about Simon and the part he plays in your life!" Now there seemed to be a certain amount of sarcasm in Robert's voice when he mentioned Simon's name.

"Then you would do as well to forget that last remark if you are insinuating that there is anything between Simon and myself!" By this time Jayne felt as if she had suffered enough with first of all Simon trying to proposition her and now Robert insinuating that there was something between them. Why wouldn't folk just leave her alone? "And what is more that is one fact that I have made clear to Simon tonight. He has been a friend to me and nothing more!"

Maybe Jayne would have stalked past her brother feeling justifiably annoyed with his insinuations but his next words stopped her dead in her tracks. "Anyway you will probably get the chance to see Luc tomorrow for he has expressed an interest in taking a look at that office you now run. After all considering that the consortium now claims to be undertaking only experimental probes in a number of places in this area at the moment, one could be forgiven for wondering what exactly that office in the town is there for!"

"I believe you are quite wrong in your assumption, the place for the drilling to take place has already been established to be in the area adjacent to the garage right here in Esprick. So why should these people want to explore other places or indeed establish an office to deal with questions on the place!"

"All I can say is that you have not been very observant of your own locale of late Jayne. Perhaps when you find the time you could cast your eyes on the field you have just quoted and point out any drilling apparatus that you see there!"

Jayne regarded him in quite a disbelievingly manner. In truth she had not been near to that field of late and consequently there were some seeds of doubt that now clouded her mind. Not that she intended to give her brother the satisfaction of knowing that he had planted them there. "Look some of us do have to work tomorrow and therefore I will leave you with your creative thoughts. Who knows you might even have concocted up some more by tomorrow!"

* * *

Robert did not see Jayne the following morning. In actuality he had decided that perhaps he had been a little hard on the girl for after all it was simply a job that she was doing up in the town and as such had nothing at all to do with the politics of the situation. Therefore he had rose early from his bed in order to apologise to her for after all this was his last day of leave and he certainly did not want to leave any ill feeling behind him when he returned to base, but in the event the girl had already left, a factor that rather gutted him.

Still he remembered that he had promised to take Luc up into the town that day, the only snag now being that whilst he was getting his things ready to depart from the house it was his mother who barraged him demanding to know where he thought he was now going on this the last day of his leave.

"Only up into town with Luc, he has expressed a desire to see it whilst he is here, who knows perhaps he has even heard of the Big One, but I will be back by lunchtime at the latest, so you see you will be able to spend some time with your son after all!"

"This man who calls himself Luc has he anything to do with the discrepancy of feelings over that portion of land?"

"You could say that considering he now owns it, an idiosyncrasy left by one of his ancestors or so I am led to believe!"

Robert was sure his mother's eyes now possessed a mark of interest in this stranger. More to the point Elaine Taylor decided that as she had not met the man for herself before this time then someone had committed a mischief towards her. "In that case why do you not bring him back here with you for after all if he is your friend then surely he must be feeling a little amiss at any obvious exclusion from your own home!"

Robert smiled at his mother's polite insistence. The woman had certainly not changed. In truth she must have spent her life looking for an angle by which she could inspire some situation that would apparently lead to her own self-aggrandisement. "Not this time Mum for time is short. Luc needs to return to Canterbury this afternoon and as for myself well I have promised to give you the benefit of my company considering I also am committed to return to my regiment tomorrow!"

"Hmmm!" It was a noise his mother often made when she realised that she was fighting a losing battle.

"So this means that this friend of yours will not be seeing Jayne even if the two of them did spend some time together in the past?"

"Perhaps they both have other interests by this time!" Robert knew full well why Luc wanted to go up into town that day and unless he was very much mistaken it was to see Jayne, but this was a factor that he was not willing to divulge at the time, more especially to the person who was listening to him. Thus it was with a kiss and a cheery goodbye that he left his mother leaving the woman to ponder on her thoughts.

⋆ ⋆ ⋆

One reason why Jayne had left early that morning was because she felt no inclination to run into her brother, or indeed anyone else from that family. Therefore she arrived in the resort far too early to open up the office. But as the morning appeared to be fair and promising after the tumults of the unpredictable weather surges of recent weeks, she decided that she would make the most of the view that served to inspire those who gazed out across the waves almost as if the waters of the ocean lapped to eternity. It was a place where many who desired to escape the claustrophobia of the inland towns came to seek a refuge; a place where gazing out to sea in this manner helped to relieve the tensions of the life that they lived, especially those who in past economic climes had worked in the mills and factories of the inland towns. Of course the resort had many other distractions for the visitor that sought to make him forget about the trials of life, such things as the 'Big one' from which one could when the wind was favourable hear their screams as its pundits scaled its dizzy heights. At this time in the day however such a feature was not yet in operation and yet there were still others who did not frequent such places and like the thing which gave them the most pleasure it was the ocean which Jayne craved with its waves that were seemingly prepared to wash away the troubles of the mind and refresh the spirit. Alas Jayne's spirit did not succumb to feeling refreshed that morning and for some reason it appeared that the well tried magic no longer was there to smooth and to calm her.

Simon's words from the previous evening still seemed to haunt her, not that she could belie herself from having let the man down lightly, but perhaps her reasons for doing so were more to the point for one person only occupied her mind and yet this person had made no effort to see her again so that she could explain that her relationship with Simon Turnbill was as nothing, let alone give her the chance to attempt to say where her true affections lay,

She was late when she finally went to open up the office. Not that this was of any consequence to her mind for after all she seldom got callers and therefore the days seemed to be long and boring confined as they were to that small square box shaped office. Yet this morning it proved to be somewhat different for no sooner had she opened that office door that one individual's sole purpose appeared to be seeking the confines of the same.

Jayne looked up at her visitor questioningly. This was someone she had not seen before, or had she? Regarding this one of stocky build who seldom mistook his twenty one units a week for water and who now appeared to have something on his mind that he was determined to share, a thought clicked open in her mind that she had indeed seen him from a distance on one prior occasion and that was when he had been talking to Simon Turnbill at the shale gas location. Now however Jayne's eyes were fixed on the pile of leaflets he carried and which he now laid down on the office table.

"I would like you to see to these leaflets being given out!" He motioned to them and upon his action Jayne sought to find out what this matter was all about. "Oh it is quite all right. I have Simon Turnbill's blessing to come here and I believe I am right in saying that it was Simon who first footed into these surrounds before hiring them out and employing yourself to look after them!" So she had been right she had spotted him in conversation with Simon before. He caught her casting yet another inquisitive eye on the parcel. "These are merely to acquaint the public of our change in venue as regards the drilling!"

Jayne gave a gasp for by this time she had already assimilated what was written on those pamphlets. "But I thought it had already been established that any drilling was to take place in Esprick by the garage? Yet in these articles you now appear to have removed the site to somewhere closer to the airport?" For a moment she did not know what to do but the other smiled on her as if treating her like some petulant child.

"I think I deserve the right to be able to move the workings to a piece of my own land which is not too far distance away and in actual fact the drilling consortium were all for having more than one string to their bow. Of course I don't suppose you yet know to whom you are speaking. The name is Stuart Bardon, so I believe that makes me your employer!" He made to take her hand and Jayne shivered for his very touch made her flesh feel creepy.

"So you are the relative of whom Luc Mathieu has spoken?" She did not know why she had mentioned Luc by his name; it was almost as if by mentioning it she was providing herself with some defence mechanism.

"I have no doubt that the bastard son of some French criminal has mentioned me. But then whether that poor apology for a man is a true relative remains to be seen. Such matters I leave to my legal representative. My concern at the moment happens to be you Miss Taylor. Simon led me to believe that you would be co-operative. I only hope that he was right in making this assumption!" His eyes were now fixed on her and Jayne could not but help notice the hardness in them. It was a look that made her feel uneasy wondering what was about to come next. But now he motioned once again to the leaflets. "I think that if you know what is good for you girl you will see that these leaflets are distributed. For the time being I will give Simon the benefit of the doubt when he said that you would prove to be helpful. I can only hope for your sake that he was right in what he said!"

Jayne was still quivering after this encounter when someone else entered the building. Her eyes lit up for a second when she saw it was Robert, but then her brother was followed close behind by another.

"I came to say farewell Sis. You disappeared out of the house this morning before I got the chance to say goodbye and therefore I followed you here: Not totally for that purpose however for Luc also expressed a desire to take a peek at the sea whilst he is in the area!" He turned to Luc before he spoke again. "Well now I have brought you to enjoy the facilities of this resort I will leave you two to it!" He moved across to give Jayne a hug. "Try and be good whilst I am away Sis and keep off my bike if you don't mind!" He cocked Luc a grin before leaving the shop without any more ado.

"Well at least I suppose it gives us the opportunity to talk!" Luc's eyes focussed on the leaflets that Stuart Bardon had left in the shop a short time before. "It appears that my relative is prepared to act fast!"

"They seem to have left the drilling site at Esprick!" She supposed it was something to say. Indeed she needed to speak before her mouth dried up altogether and she hoped that by thinking of something to say this would halt the tell-tale burning in her cheeks.

"And you are left to spread the message?"

"That is not true. If you had been here a minute earlier you would have witnessed their arrival at the hands of your cousin!"

"The fact that he arrived with such trickery does not surprise me. But forgetting my relatives for one moment Jayne I think that you and I need to talk. Consequently I suggest you close up this shop which is doing nobody any good and then we will be able to have some free time to ourselves!"

Jayne looked at him for a moment. Of course what he had said made sense. The shop had been quiet enough before and now Stuart Bardon had placed himself at the centre of things she did not want to know anymore. Still Luc Mathieu still provided an assault on her senses!

"Give me the key then and I will lock up!" The man in front of her was beginning to get impatient and Jayne handed him the object without second thoughts.

Luc stood by the front door with a look of determination in his eyes as she collected her things together and then when she passed by him he locked the door with some determination before pocketing the key.

"That is the last time you will be working here. Now get into the car please!" He motioned her to where he had parked the vehicle yet his face still contained a certain hardness and Jayne endeavouring to do his wishes moved across to the vehicle conscious as she did so of the seagulls squawking overhead. For a moment she almost envied them for they possessed the freedom to be able to fly to their heart's content whilst she herself seemed always to be bound by the complexities of life.

He held the door open for her to get in but that was the last of the niceties she was to observe at that time for Luc drove in silence almost indeed as if he wished to relieve the tension that had built up inside of him. And thus in the light of the morning sun Jayne observed the resort coming to life as they motored down the promenade for now visitors having partaken of their breakfasts were beginning to filter into the streets no doubt anxious to experience for themselves the ethos that made this place tick and perhaps even be the first to note various aspects of the town which they could confidently relate to their contemporaries.

And yet Luc still remained silent and as they left the piers behind them Jayne began to wonder where they were heading for. It was on the outskirts of that resort by the lake in the place which prided itself as being upmarket to its nearest rival that Luc finally stopped.

"I considered that we both needed the time to cool down!" Perhaps the words were an explanation for his silence and yet his expression was still terse. "But shall we get one thing clear and that is you are not going back to that place. Whoever it is who leases that property can come for the key to me if they so wish!"

"But Simon-----?" She did not know what made her bring his name into it unless she was still seeking for some defensive mechanism against this person who had the ability to numb her senses.

"Blow Simon and I for one would be obliged if we could leave that man's name out of it for I am no longer prepared to cow tow to one who is not above suspicion himself. Your brother told me that you had received a summons to attend the trial of Jules Mathieu in order to give evidence?"

She nodded still wondering what Luc was getting at.

"I doubt if such proceedings will be held in this part of the country and therefore after due consideration I have decided that perhaps the best way all around is for you to come back with me to Priory Manor!"

"You mean just like that?"

"That is exactly what I mean which is why I intend to drive in that direction now!"

"But surely I cannot go anywhere without first making arrangements!" She tried to moisten her lips with her tongue but found this to be a difficult task. "For starters I need to go home in order to collect my things!"

"You can and what is more to the point you will come with me without further argument. Perhaps you have forgotten the wardrobe which is full of your things that you left behind at Priory Manor when you previously left in what appeared to be one almighty hurry; therefore I do not deem it necessary for you to return to collect any of your belongings. Furthermore I want no outcry from your mother or arguments why you should not go! That is possibly the reason why I have kidnapped you Jayne for I have no intention of letting you go back now." If he wondered at her consequent silence and if he had turned his head to look at her he would have noticed her imminent surrender for the beating of her heart had now put paid to any further objections. All she could do was to be thankful that her true feelings were not quite as obvious. "Can I take it then from your silence that you are now in agreement with me?"

It was not her agreement about travelling to Priory Manor immediately that had held Jayne's tongue but rather because she had finally realised why her heart kept pumping so loudly and at the time she had no way of knowing whether such feelings were reciprocated from this person, the only clue to his feelings being the way his fingers gnashed into the dashboard

"You have not yet replied, but then Jayne you were always the one who liked to make a mystery out of matters. Therefore I will take your silence as that of agreeing with me. And now I suggest that we drive further and shake off any remnants of this mordant feeling before we look for somewhere to eat!"

He started up the car and as the coastline began to fade behind her Jayne could not help but wonder what now lay ahead.

They had left Lancashire far behind circumnavigating the Pennines whilst Jayne mused upon this ridge of mountains that now appeared to separate her from all that was familiar. before Luc finally stopped outside of a Little Chef. "Your lunch break; well I consider that it is time that we ate for after all we do not want to arrive back at Priory Manor feeling on the point of starvation or Mrs Bentham will certainly have something to say!"

She made to follow him into the place as if in a dream. Indeed she must have still been in something of a trance otherwise she would have seen the step she eventually stumbled over. But Luc had noticed her actions foolish as they were and it was his arms that came out to prevent her from falling and leaning close against him she was aware of his sweet smell of masculinity from which she no longer wished to be parted from.

It was then that he kissed her; tentatively at first perhaps anxious as to how she would respond. But he needn't have had any fears over her reaction to his assault. Instead her lips met his own willingly as she clung ever closer to his body as if this provided her with the aphrodisiac she sought to nurture her senses.

“I’m sorry!” Something innate within her told her that it was time to break away despite her emotions of that time.

“Why should you be sorry?” He glanced at her in a quizzical manner and for a moment she forgot her inbred desire to do the right thing and that was not to force herself on Luc Mathieu. “Perhaps instead you should be glad that such an action helped to break the tension that lies between us. Please don’t say that you are not aware of the magnetic situation that lies between us! Perhaps we need to talk about this once the time is more opportune!”

She supposed that he spoke the words of common sense but then at that moment in time common sense over the matter seemed to go only a small way to satisfy the need she felt within her and something in Luc’s eyes now told her that once the time was opportune there would be much more to say!

Chapter Ten

Jayne had fully expected Mrs Bentham to have given one of her customary sniffs upon their arrival at the Manor, but today the woman appeared to be on her best behaviour. In fact she actually greeted Jayne with a half-smile which made the girl wonder, at least for a moment, what scheme the woman was correctly hatching out in her head. Still the woman's initial words served to dispel some of the girl's fears.

"Welcome back to Priory Manor Miss Taylor. I guess you have been missed around here!"

Upon these words Jayne tried to catch Luc's eye but provocatively the man had now turned away as he issued his introductory statement. "Miss Taylor will be staying here with us until at least after the court hearing at the very earliest!"

The housekeeper nodded in response and Jayne swore she must surely have been wrong when she spotted a twinkle in the woman's eye. "Aye well such matters often take their time but in the meantime Miss I'm sure we will be glad of your company. I guess the Master here has been behaving like a bear with a sore head ever since you left us the last time. Well I guess I've never really met a bear with a sore head but if the master's behaviour is anything to go by then I am glad that I haven't!" Jayne glanced in Luc's direction. It somehow gave her spirits a lift by hearing that he had apparently missed her and he had not after all invented some yarn on the matter. Still the housekeeper seemed to be still a little concerned. "I guess that I need to apologise though for I had no idea that you were coming today and therefore I am afraid that I have not prepared a meal for you!" The woman now looked as if she had done something wrong.

"We have already eaten on the way down!" It was Luc who now endeavoured to put the woman at her ease. "Besides I know full well that Tuesday happens to be your Bingo night therefore there is literally no reason why you should not follow your leisure pursuits. If Jayne or I do happen to feel hungry then we are quite capable of raiding your fridge!"

Somehow with this response Jayne gathered that Luc now wanted the woman off the premises at least for a while, a thought which once again sent quivers to her heart.

"Well if you are quite sure Sir although it doesn't seem right for me to go off in that manner when supposedly I should be caring for you!"

"Guess you will be too late to partake in the first game if you don't make a speedy exit Mrs Bentham!"

The woman looked graciously at her boss before donning the coat hung up downstairs. "I guess I had better go then! You two will be all right, won't you?"

"Of course we will Mrs Bentham and what is more we promise that the house will be the same as it was on you return for we have no intention of holding any wild parties whilst you are away!"

The two watched Mrs Bentham leave in her own indomitable fashion, hesitant and still not totally convinced that she was doing the right thing and as they watched Jayne became conscious of Luc's arm resting on her shoulders.

"Well I guess that fate has fallen exactly into our own hands all of which reminds me that there is still something which is waiting to be aired between us. What exactly did you mean Jayne when you kissed me earlier on today?"

Jayne drew in a deep breath. She could no longer deny Luc even to herself. But Luc gave her little time to explain. "Perhaps we ought to subject ourselves once again and resume that kiss and see if we can discern exactly what is going on?" He did not wait for a reply for the next moment Jayne felt herself swept up into his arms whilst his lips positively raped her own. Nor did Jayne offer any resistance to this onslaught. Instead she now used her lips to further invite him as she became drunk by the passion which was exuded.

"I said that we had things to sort out between us!" He finally reminded her as he came up for air and then realising that he had met no resistance. "And perhaps now the time is more opportune for us to do just that!"

His hand clenched her wrist as they mounted the stairs at the Priory and there now could be little doubt as to where he was leading her. But Jayne was a willing participant for her body still marvelled at his closeness and she wondered just how many times in the past she had yearned to be in this position. The bedroom door yielded little opposition as they passed through into that room and it was with tenderness that he finally deposited her on the bed.

"Guess this is something which we need to settle right here and now!" He murmured the words as she saw him loosen his clothing but by this time Jayne was already ahead of him for surely this was her desire. After all she wanted this man, she needed his infinite closeness and she was therefore a willing participant when Luc took her for his own.

It was later as she lay on the bed feeling completely satiated and full of love for the man to whom she had willingly given herself that she noticed Luc seemed to be deep in thought, almost indeed as if his actions had now awoken the desire for a permanency in this new found relationship.

"Tell me, do you want to marry from home or shall we get a special licence and marry here?"

His words surprised her, she had expected to feel his body yet again but now the man appeared to be having some sort of repercussions on his action. Perhaps her silence evoked some understanding of her present emotions for he bent over her to stroke her face, almost as if he felt the need to convince her that the words he now uttered were heartfelt. "I do want to marry you, I guess I did long before today but now I can hide my feelings no longer!"

Her heart filled with an abundance of joy upon hearing these words. Of course she wanted to marry him, to spend the rest of her life with him, but now the thought of her mother's reaction to a wedding, any wedding in fact which involved her daughter, appeared to promote an hesitancy in her response and filled her with dismay.

"Of course I will marry you Luc, with all of my heart; but not from home I pray for my mother's reaction to such an event would only serve to spoil our day!"

"In that case I will see about getting a special license tomorrow Jayne and we will marry from Priory Manor. All I want is your happiness for I love you so very much and I regard myself as a fool for not recognising it earlier!"

Her hands came up to stroke his face. "Guess we have been pretty busy with other things of late!"

"Not a sufficient excuse and something that I swear I will spend the rest of my life trying to make up to you!" His lips found hers again and now there was time for no more words as their bodies became entwined once more and they allowed true love to become their master!

⋆ ⋆ ⋆

"I thought that I had made myself perfectly clear when I told you to deal with that girl!" The face of the older man seemed to be almost contorted into resembling an object from a horror movie as he faced his companion. For his part Simon Turnbill found himself colouring up as he searched for the right words to respond to this unwarranted outburst, for it had after all been unexpected and consequently words in response seemed to be difficult to find.

"Believe you me I have tried to cultivate her!" Perhaps his words finally emerged like some strangled admission of defeat; something which did not altogether please his accuser.

"You tried to cultivate her! You might have done better if you had chosen to finish her off permanently.

"Her mother was my ally in this for she was all for our relationship and at least if I had married Jayne it would have sort of removed her from the equation for if this had been the case then I am sure that solicitor of yours could have found enough on that man Mathieu to make him relinquish any claim he thought he had on the land which lies in close proximity to her home. Following on from that, with the purchase of the Hall settled Mathieu could then have returned to his native France with money in his pocket!"

"Sometimes I get the impression that you are a dimwit Turnbill! How on earth you ever managed to get yourself involved with banking I cannot possibly hazard a guess unless that was you were helped into that position possibly through the influence of some family connections!"

"Casting such aspersions on my family will not serve to solve your problem at this stage!" Simon tried to draw himself up tall but only succeeded in making himself resemble more of a walrus than an executive. Still his words seemed to have made some impression on the other man.

"Maybe I concede that you do have a point in what you say but even so you will still be assisting me in my next move!"

"Which is, if I dare pose such a question?" Simon Turnbill finally managed to regain a little of his former composure

The other man looked at him almost as if he was in some pain at having to explain such tactics. "This new solicitor that Mathieu employed in an effort to discredit my claim; I believe that he is quite new to the job and therefore in all likelihood he will require money in order to get himself established. I feel sure that you will be able to persuade your bank that he will be a worthy client for them to invest in, always providing of course that he is willing to do the right thing by us! After all I am sure that there must be some obscure clause in that will which when scrutinised thoroughly could throw its legality into doubt!"

"Then you are asking me to persuade this man to lie?"

"I feel that the word lie is perhaps a little too strong a word to use when dealing in legal circles Simon. After all a solicitor can be said to be devious without him actually lying, especially if the rewards for doing this are made substantial!"

"But what if the Bank refuses to play ball with this arrangement?"

"Really Simon, I was given to understand that you are in charge of investment therefore I do not imagine that it will be too difficult for you to persuade your employers to see matters through your eyes. After all you have used your persuasive powers before in the past; I could name the Taylors by name if I had to in order to bring matters closer to home. Therefore I do not think I am expecting too much of you if I say that I expect you to proceed with the matter in hand without further delay. After all one must consider that it is costing me money to pay rental on that land simply in order to keep the drillers within the area and I do believe that now even they are beginning to regard me rather suspiciously! The crux of the matter is that I want that land Turnbill, the acreage that is there which could make me a fortune and which I feel that I was cheated out of by that Frenchman. Do you now understand me?"

"I will see what I can do!" The younger man still seemed to be far too reticent in his response for Bardon who in turn practically snarled viciously back at the young man.

"Never mind seeing what you can do, just do it Turnbill and that I repeat is an order!"

Sitting in that ante chamber with its walls uninspiringly decorated with a coat of distemper whilst its furnishings left something to be desired if ever one could be persuaded to call the place comfortable, Jayne reflected that this Tuesday must surely be one that could go down on record. Indeed now looking down the corridor which led to this place she was beginning to wonder how on earth she had allowed herself to be talked into using this venue, which one could consider was hardly the place that most young brides dreamt of.

The day had begun in court and the fact that Luc had been by her side at the time had done little to ease the chagrin she felt when her evidence proved to be enough to place Luc's own father behind bars. Luc had assured her that he certainly did not mind this outcome, indeed he stated that the world might well be a better place after that man was incarcerated away, but then the prisoner in the dock upon whom she had been called to give evidence against was Luc's father which to Jayne's eyes threw a completely different perspective on the matter.

She had noted that all through those proceedings Luc had been referring to his watch for there was a later appointment they had to attend which was of far more interest to him than the offender whom he had never known as his father and who indeed had done his only son few favours. Perhaps it was unfortunate that both engagements were on the same day. It had certainly not been planned that way initially, but then the legal profession appeared to be in a position to demand one's presence whatever other arrangements one had made for that particular time.

Consequently it had proved to be something of a rush when those proceedings were finally over with in order to get to this second venue. Of course Mrs Bentham had been waiting for them there and was now attempting to ooze pleasantries from her lips and words of re-assurance. But then of course it was necessary for Mrs Bentham to be there for at this appointment Luc and Jayne required two witnesses, and because the two had craved no fuss Mrs Bentham had proved to be the perfect choice for one of those witnesses more especially when she had managed to rope in one of her male bingo playing friends to stand as the second witness. Thus as the housekeeper now offered her re-assurances and even presented Jayne with a bouquet of local flowers, Jayne's fixation had been on the décor of this nondescript building.

Perhaps indeed for one moment Jayne had wondered whether she would have been far better after all to have married from home for this place presented nothing of the feeling that a wedding should inspire. Instead the place was clinically flat something that only some government civil service would have adhered to in the philosophy of performing this function with the least possible effort apart from that which was placed into writing out the marriage certificate. Yet the thought of a marriage from home was something that she quickly dispelled for although Jayne would have welcomed some sort of special feeling the thought of what a marriage with her mother in fawning attendance would have entailed made this nondescript affair all the more tempting.

Looking at Luc's expression as he waited his turn to enter the room of sanctimonial rites she watched as he glanced at his watch as if he was wondering how much longer they would be kept waiting in this building which certainly needed replacing in the twenty first century and she concluded that his thoughts on this place were akin to her own. Only Mrs Bentham now appeared to be excited with the ceremony that was about to be enacted, but then of course the whole experience was still new to the woman who sought now only to please after expressing her delight at being asked. Her partner that day however may have made the promise to be in attendance but was now showing signs that this interlude was already beginning to interfere with his game of Bingo, and as the jackpot had reached a new level in its rollover his only thoughts were that someone might possibly win this before he could return in order to take part.

Finally however they were called to pass inside into the holy of holies, Jayne did wonder for a moment what had happened to the bride and groom who had gone in before them. The girl had been dressed very differently to Jayne for she had worn the full white regalia, despite the fact that according to her physique the girl was possibly ready to drop at any moment.

"There is another door to exit by!" Mrs Bentham decided to share her wisdom no doubt now assuming that this fact needed to be made known. "It leads into a courtyard where one can take photographs! Therefore the chances are you won't be seeing her again for after the ceremony no doubt the pair will want to take full advantage of this facility!"

Jayne had never thought of photographs on this occasion but obviously Mrs Bentham had because she now lost no time in producing a camera which, she determined, would hang over her arm during the proceedings. Not that Jayne had any qualms about where Mrs Bentham would display this object for her main criterion as she stood before making her way into that inner sanctum was whether her dress was creased and whether after all she should have taken the time to have left the stable in order to purchase something perhaps a little more suited to the occasion.

Once on her feet she glanced in Luc's direction however and the expression which was now obvious in the man's eyes made her forget all about the clothes she wore and others she would now have liked to have replaced them with not to mention the dinginess of this place for surely the most important thing was that the two of them were here to be finally joined in matrimony. Thinking only of these things Jayne was barely conscious of the words issued in that place for the voice of the registrar seemed to drone on as if in perpetuity almost as I the woman was issuing forth some sleeping draught and therefore she was glad that Mrs Bentham was close at hand and there to guide her into making her responses at the correct time.

Nobody seemed to regard the antics of Mrs Bentham's friend from the bingo hall as being significant and as for the man himself, he was only too pleased to get the task he had unwittingly allowed himself to be talked into over and done with, upon which, after first signing the register as a witness to the act, then obliged everyone by disappearing from off the set at a speed which would have even surprised the heavens.

The fact however that Luc had decided to take Jayne away somewhere directly after the wedding had not however deterred Mrs Bentham for that person had decided that a wedding breakfast was now in order and had indeed worked her socks off to make preparations for such an affair before she had left Priory Manor earlier that day. Thus it was with a feeling of pride that the woman faced the couple after the ceremony was over and Jayne and Luc had themselves found themselves abandoned in that quadrangle which others used for photography, and announced the same to them.

If they were surprised, and Jayne for her part would have preferred somewhere far more conducive to photography that this quadrangle, then at least they had the good manners not to throw the whole idea back into the face of this woman who had only sought to do what was right and thus before the two newlyweds found themselves returning to Priory Manor, they posed whilst the woman clicked her camera shutter open; if only to partake in the effort Mrs Bentham had made.

Yet Luc was anxious to be away for now he resented sharing his new bride with anyone and that even included Mrs Bentham. Therefore after the preliminaries were over he made his grand announcement that they had a train to catch.

Jayne looked at him slightly puzzled for she had no idea about this and in response he smiled gently down at her. “Surely I am to be allowed to take my new wife away for a few days on her honeymoon?”

If Jayne was agog at the news Mrs Bentham was obviously anxious to hear more. "Then where are you going? You never mentioned going away!"

"Isn't it the customary thing to do after a wedding or do the English not extend to this sort of practise and is it not usual for the destination to remain a closely guarded secret?"

"Then how long will you be away for?"

"Perhaps a fortnight or so this time around, although I must confess that I will be looking to taking Jayne to somewhere far more exotic before the year is out. Don't worry Mrs Bentham you can take the time off for I will contact you when we are ready to return! Just think about that bingo jackpot!"

It was Jayne who made to kiss the woman before they left and to thank her for all that she had done on their behalf and the older woman looked up at her this time without the sniffs but with a genuine smile on her face!

In the event Luc took Jayne to France to show her the countryside where he had been brought up as well as the châteaux where his mother had been compelled to seek work even when he had been little more than a baby. And then so as not to dwell for too long on the more sordid matters in his earlier life, Luc took her on to Paris, the place often described as the city of true love.

Thus Jayne and Luc travelled to Paris where he was fully determined to show her the love of a true Frenchman, perhaps the only thing of being French of which he now felt proud, and after they mused around the sights where Jayne could appreciate the true culture of that city and wished that the time in that place would never end.

Still that was not to be for during their second week Luc questioned her on whether she had let her mother know that they were married. "After all she has a right to know I suppose and at least there is little that she can do about it now!"

"I will phone her when I get back. At the moment I resent spoiling our time here for anything!"

He was silent after her response and it was then that Jayne realised that he himself had already had thoughts of going back to Priory Manor. "After all it is a new life there for both of us and no doubt we will have a great deal of sorting out to do in order to make it our home!"

She nodded her agreement reticently for after all Luc was right, their honeymoon, as delightful as it had been, could not possibly last for ever. "Then don't forget you promised to contact Mrs Bentham before our return. After all she would never forgive you if she happened to be out playing bingo when we returned!"

He kissed her then, a deep passionate kiss that sent its vibes to her very soul and did not seem to realise that they were still out in the street at the time. Well after all, Paris was supposed to be the city of love so who on earth could possibly object to this action!

* * *

They had only been back at the Manor for a couple of days and Jayne had still not got around to informing her mother of her new status when they had an unexpected visitor in the shape of Alistair Dennett who wore a face that appeared dour and serious as he practically begged Mrs Bentham, who had opened the door to him, to see Luc.

"He's actually in the study at the moment trying to sort some things out!" Jayne had heard his voice from the hall and knowing how the young man had previously helped Luc she interjected and invited him inside. "Go through if you like, it is Alistair isn't it?"

The young man nodded in response to her question but as that expression of seriousness still girded his face Jayne began to wonder what was wrong for as far as she knew all the legalities surrounding the Manor had now been dealt with. Indeed perhaps it was with this knowledge in mind that Jayne made to follow the young solicitor and noticing her at the study door Luc had no hesitation in telling her to come in as well.

"I have no secrets from my wife so whatever it is you have to say I would prefer her to be present. Indeed all things relating to the Manor are hers as much as my own!"

"In that case I am afraid that I have some news that I have to impart to you which does not exactly make for pleasant hearing!" Perhaps the young solicitor thought that Luc would think better about Jayne being present on this but instead Luc motioned him to a chair for even though their previous acquaintanceship had been only of a short duration the Lord of the Manor certainly felt that he could both trust and felt perfectly at ease with this young advocate of the law.

"I am afraid that I have to report that your relatives have recently been seeking to cause trouble for you!" The young man finally spoke his words slowly as if he wished to allow the gist of what he was talking about time to sink in and as a result it was Luc who now regarded him through eyes that were stretched wide as he had already determined that such people as Stuart Bardon could now be dispelled and buried into the background in a cesspit of their own making!

"As a matter of fact there has been an attempt to bribe me into finding some sort of outlandish clause in the will of Edward Bardon which could subject your claim to this place to further scrutiny!" The young man had been trained well in his profession and thus he made his words stretch out which served to confuse the listener even though this was without malice of forethought.

"And --?" The young lawyer's rhetoric had obviously succeeded in completely throwing Luc off his guard.

"No doubt you will be relieved to know that I told the bearer of such potential gifts which he considered relevant in order to buy my compliance exactly where he could go for I feel confident that there never was any such clause and neither am I persuaded into adopting the role of perjury even for considerable monetary gain. What is more I think that you should also know that I have now decided to proceed and report this incident to the relevant authorities. Therefore as it is your property which lies at the heart of this devious scheme I felt that I had no alternative but to acquaint you with the facts especially if further proceedings are now to ensue!"

"In that case I believe that I owe you a debt of gratitude!" Luc now nodded sombrely in the young lawyer's direction. "I can take it then from our conversation that it is my cousin who is seeking to cause trouble?"

"Your cousin Stuart Bardon is involved in this matter yes but the puppet he sent to me outlining such demands also claimed that he was a banker in his own right. Something that possibly suggests that their monetary funding would be readily available providing I had agreed to their suggestion!"

Luc heard a gasp coming from Jayne's lips at the mention of this banker and his immediate reaction was now to protect his wife therefore he stretched out his arms to bid her to come and sit besides him. "You said that you presumed that your minnow was a banker of some description?" Now he felt that he had to voice this question if only for Jayne's sake.

"He answered to the name of Simon Turnbill!" The words were finally out and now there could be no disguising the fact of who this banker was. "Of course I am under no illusion that the man was anything other than some minnow sent to reconnoitre for your cousin. Indeed that was the reason why I gave both names to the authorities. By doing this I do not consider that I have exceeded my own role in this matter Mr Mathieu!"

"I consider that you did exactly right Mr Dennett!" Luc at least afforded the man a smile on these words even if his head was pounding at the time over what had been said. "As a matter of fact my wife and I are both well acquainted with both individuals in question and we fully agree with your judgement on the matter. Indeed I consider that it will be more than satisfactory for the law to be left to deal with the pair and their obvious misdemeanours. And now Mr Dennett I am sure that you will take afternoon tea with us otherwise you will only serve to upset my housekeeper!"

Mrs Bentham made her appearance almost before Luc had time to ring the bell to summons her. No doubt the woman had been doing her best to listen in to what was going on. But then of course that was Mrs Bentham's trademark but then after the recent kindness that has been shown her by this woman Jayne would not stoop to condemn her action. Thus tea was to be served in what might have appeared to be a ridiculous situation to any outsider but which as far as Mrs Bentham was concerned was a product of good manners and etiquette

Jayne realised the she had not yet phoned her mother to confirm that she was now a married woman despite her promise to Luc that she would do so. Her reasons for not doing so had centred on the fact of the thought of the reception she would get upon this declaration, the wailing and gnashing of teeth which would not make for pleasant listening down the telephone. Still she was fully aware that she had already promised Luc that she would do so and now he had plenty of other things to worry about besides her relationship with her mother. Thus she finally decided that perhaps enough time had elapsed and therefore it was time for her to take the bull by the horns. Thus stealing herself after the evening meal that night to make that call she was quite surprised when her own mobile shrilled out that someone wished to contact her and upon picking up the phone it was to find that the woman she had in mind to ring was already on the end of that line.

"Jayne something terrible has happened!" Such an opening was so like her mother for titbits of information often held priority in her eyes over one's well-being. "Guess what, I have just heard that Simon Turnbill has been arrested on some trumped up charge!"

"For once I do believe that you have heard right Mum!"

"But why: Why do you think I am right? Whatever can have happened? After all Simon is such a nice young man with a promising future in front of him. You know full well that I had him in mind for you!"

"Well that is something that you don't need to worry about any further Mum although I thought you were aware that I turned Simon Turnbill down simply yonks' ago, that is if he ever really existed in my life. I also believe that he was involved with others whose sole efforts lay in scheming to cheat innocent parties. But there is something else which you also need to know. I just happen to be a married woman now therefore any further entreaties on your part which favour Simon could now be considered to be misguided!"

"Are my ears deceiving me? You can't possibly be married otherwise you would have told us sooner for you know Jayne that I always wanted the perfect wedding for you, here in the village church, and anyway if you have not married Simon who on earth have you married?"

Jayne had been expecting some form of garble from her mother's lips in response, but then she conceded, the woman had obviously had a shock with her declaration and therefore she spoke her next words to the woman gently, hoping that she could make her understand.

"I married Luc, Mum! We had a quiet wedding for that was what we both wanted and as we were both passed the age of consent we did not need anyone's permission to get married the way we wanted to. After that Luc took me to France to see the place where he was raised and then we went on to Paris. Still we are back now and living at Priory Manor------!"

"But you never let me know?"

"I was going to ring you tonight Mum but you managed to race me to the phone!"

"I don't know what your father will have to say about all of this. For years he has geared himself up to having one day to give away his daughter and now you have completely spoiled the occasion for him. What are the neighbours going to say about it too?"

"Does it really matter what they say?"

"Of course it matters. We will be made to feel like laughing stocks in the village around here. Simon was so worried when you disappeared, and not only that but he couldn't get into his office up in town for you apparently had the key!"

"But Luc made a point of sending him the key to that place. I remember when he put it into an envelope and then posted it to you!"

"Well I can assure you that Simon was worried before he received it. But I tried to contact you Jayne, I rang your number so many times, I left messages but you never replied!"

"I guess I forgot to take my mobile on my honeymoon with me!" She hadn't forgotten of course for she had deliberately left it behind and although she hated herself for telling a lie she now deemed that it was necessary. "Anyway it sounds as if Simon has far more to worry about now!"

"I wish I knew just what was going on for Simon is such a good boy. He has helped your father and me with our investments you know!"

Jayne did know, not that she was for enlightening her mother any further and worrying her at the moment with anything else. "Look Mum, I will have to go now, Luc has quite a lot of business to sort out down here but I am sure that when he is able we will take a trip back to see you!" She guessed that it was the only way she could end this conversation. Of course she knew her mother would soon be back on the phone again now she had caught her and Luc exuded sympathy when he saw her expression.

"So I guess you have finally done the deed and now you feel like a complete eel?" His arms snaked around her neck as his lips muzzled through her hair. "Things will be all right with your parents in the long run so try not to worry for our bigger concern right now is what is happening around here!"

It must surely have been designed by the gods that during their stay in France Luc and Jayne had not run into Stuart Bardon, for that man, now positively furious concerning the negative results after an attempt had been made to bribe Alistair Dennett had decided on his own initiative to visit the place where Luc Mathieu had spent his childhood in an attempt to unravel some sordid detail about that family which would prove useful to him in his claim or the estate which had now been dismissed by the British courts. In truth he did not know what he expected to find, indeed one could say that it was one last desperate effort from a man who now felt he was on the verge of losing far too much. This time around however he had not taken Simon Turnbill into his confidence for in all truth he was beginning to view that one as a complete bore as well as proving that he was useless to him.

Therefore Stuart Bardon arrived at Luc's home town just after the two had left for Paris and had thus spared them some unpleasantries. Perhaps Bardon was there searching not so much for evidence of Luc's own life but that of Luc's father and therefore it became far easier for him to inveigle his way into a caucus of some of Jules Mathieu's contemporaries. One thing however he soon was made aware of and that was that Jules Mathieu had not been held in high regard by his contemporaries. Indeed far from it for the man in question had been quite prepared to steal from this group in order to suit his own purpose. Not that after looking at this caucus with some care Bardon did not entirely fault the other man for stealing from them but the fact that Mathieu had possessed the audacity to cheat them still filled these people with a sense of hatred against him. Therefore after working out his scheme meticulously, Bardon found that he now had a number of new minnows who could be now bribed into carrying out certain tasks for him especially when these related to the family of Jules Mathieu's descendants.

"Tell me something mon amie how are you with women?"

The eyes of the one to whom he was speaking lit up for after all he considered that all Frenchmen were capable of dealing with women. "You question me Monsieur, a born Frenchman?"

"The one whom I have in mind possibly holds the strings to the present younger Mathieu's success and I do believe that if she was removed from the scene then Luc Mathieu himself would soon capitulate!"

The young Frenchman looked puzzled for he felt that he required far more information on this matter than what had emerged so far. That was when Stuart Bardon placed his wallet containing a substantial amount of Euros down on the table. "If you should successfully abduct this woman whom I feel now stands in the way of me being able to claim my own rights, then this amount will be yours!"

"You are asking us to kill this person then?"

"No I do not envisage such things for kill to my ears sounds an ugly word. I merely wish for you to remove her from the scene for a time until after legal niceties have been sorted out!"

"You have picture of this girl?"

Stuart Bardon fished in his pocket and produced a rather crumpled up likeness of Jayne; a photograph that he had managed to obtain from Simon Turnbill in one of his better moments.

"The girl is attractive enough not to kill that I agree, where then am I likely to find this fille?"

"At a place called Priory Manor, which is an estate that lies just outside of Canterbury!"

"Then she also comes with a silver spoon in her mouth, what would you have me do with her?"

"That my friend is your business except there is one thing and that is once my transaction to receive my rightful inheritance is settled I expect her to be returned in the same manner as which you find her!"

The one to whom he was speaking then reached out a hand his sole intention now to lay his fingers on the wallet that still lay on the table but Bardon shook his head.

"You will receive payment on completion of this mission!" The express on his face was enough to deter even the most ardent of adversaries.

"Half now and half on completion. Those are my terms!"

Bardon hesitated before realising that he now had little alternative if he wished the task to be completed and then fished amongst the money, half of which he then returned to his wallet.

"Then we have a deal but remember the girl will not be returned until the second payment is received!"

Bardon could do little else but agree although he left the place feeling that at least he had got things moving in his way. It was the English newspaper on the news stand that then arrested his attention, for the headlines referred to the arrest of the man he knew as Simon Turnbill for embezzlement and also with the additional headlines that the police were additionally looking for a second person in connection with this case and Bardon scowled, for if that Pratt started to sing then it would only be a question of time before the authorities were chasing him. Therefore the only way he could avoid such an interruption to his plans was for him to remain here in France in the hopes that no one recognised him for Stuart Bardon was determined that he was not going to give up the chase at this stage!

Chapter Eleven

The place was sparse if indeed functional with its lack of decoration and furnished only with the rows of identical tables each of which housed two chairs one on either side of the table and which were not intended to offer any degree of comfort for those who wished to ease their frame into them. But then Jules Matthieu had to reluctantly admit that things could have been a great deal worse if he had been considered to be a violent man and had thus been forced to park his frame behind one of those large unbreakable glass screens and entertain his visitor from one side of this barricade which offered little privacy. Not it may be said that Jules Matthieu had expected to receive any visitors whilst he was incarcerated within this prison. Indeed the surprise had been his when he had been summoned to attend this place that was set aside for visitors. Yet the name of his visitor that had been recited to him was that of a person he had known well in the past whilst he had been in France and therefore this person who was visiting was not of English origin and therefore perhaps it was more out of curiosity than anything else that had persuaded him to agree to receive this visitor.

He spotted the stance of Renee Pascal sitting at one of these tables as the guards allowed him to enter this room from the confines of the inner prison even though one of their number was keeping a watchful eye on events that transpired during this short time when prisoners were allowed to receive such visitors and furthermore such watchful eyes were there not only to spot anything amiss which might happen within these quarters but also to monitor that nothing was passed to the prisoner and that the hands of both prisoner and visitor were kept firmly to their own side of the table. Neither was the time allotted long in its duration and therefore prisoners were expected to exchange greetings with their visitor in the briefest possible time.

"You came to see me?" Jules' voice still held a note of incredulity in it as he made to sit down in the space which was allotted to him.

"Of course you are an old friend, am I not right in saying this?"

"But how did you find out that I was here?" The man was still puzzled. Rene Pascal was from France therefore Jules began to wonder how he had discovered that he was here, let alone the reason for this visit, which was something which he could not fully comprehend. This of course was in addition to the fact that Jules Matthieu had not entirely been bosom friends with the Frenchman in the past.

"I myself had a visitor; a person who was prepared to go to great lengths in order to find me. This person appeared to be extremely upset by matters that had recently arisen concerning your son. In actual fact I was more than surprised to hear that you had such a thing as an offspring for you have never mentioned anything about this one in the past!"

"I never considered the matter to be relevant. So you are telling me that you have decided to visit me because of my son?"

"In a way that is true. The Englishman who came to see me appeared to be under the impression that your son had cheated him out of his inheritance. That was when I decided that the person of whom he spoke must indeed be your son, for such tendencies appear to be a family trait. Not of course that I would have anticipated such a visit especially from of all things an Englishman but in all truth my visitor, as well as being upset at what appeared to have befallen him also proved to have a generous heart towards anyone willing to assist him! My visit here is therefore to qualify your feelings on the matter if we should decide it is necessary to despatch your kith and kin, for apparently your son can be most stubborn on matters very much as you are yourself and is therefore not adept in the power of being able to reason!"

"I have several sons. Of which one do you now speak?"

"The one whom I believe you already know inherited the estate which lies not so many miles away from where we are today!"

"What of him? I myself have few feelings about the one of whom you speak except to state that it is mainly due to his efforts that I now find myself here incarcerated in this soulless place which only the English could design!"

"My associate believes that his claim to this inheritance was unlawful and therefore the one who has caused my mentor so much trouble in recent days should be persuaded to go back to France where he was born, by force if necessary!"

"And I believed that you cared for our motherland! What has France done to deserve the return of this half breed and how are you going to persuade him to return? You mentioned something about despatching the fellow?"

"A strong word I agree, but then there is more than one way of despatching some undesirable. I believe the one of whom we speak has now acquired himself a wife, a pretty filly or so I am given to understand!"

"So what is this to me?" Still the memory of Jayne Matthieu or whatever she liked to call herself remained fast in his memory. Yes she was a pretty filly, maybe he himself would have welcomed the opportunity to make the woman squirm. After all he had done that to others and he was not yet past the age when he could vilify them. For a moment he wished he was out of this place for if there was any vilification to be done then he would have welcomed such an opportunity.

"Maybe we could force the young pretender to give up any claim to the posh set up he appears to have acquired and return to France by using the girl to the best advantage. After all from all accounts your son appears to be besotted by her!"

"Then for once my son appears to have shown good taste. Yet I fail to understand why you are telling me all this for whatever happens to the girl appears to be out of my jurisdiction at the moment!"

"The girl happens to be your own daughter in law. Therefore it could be said that it goes beyond the realms of fantasy that you would not like to see her come to any physical harm. Therefore I might suggest that the girl might indeed be despatched out of the country of her birth!"

"And what is this to me?"

"If the man whom she married is so besotted with the wench then surely it is more likely that he will be inclined to rescind his ownership of both the property and the land he has acquired in this country in order to see the girl again. If this is the case then I am also sure that my superior, who himself is not without influence, will see that you are also released from this most unwarranted situation you now find yourself in!"

"And if my bastard son chooses to flex his mussels and declares that the prospect of his entitlement in England far exceeds his need for a wife?"

"I have every confidence in how you will treat this foreign filly once you are back again in France if her husband has no further use for her!"

A bell rang signalling that the time for the visits had past and Renee Pascal stood. "I would offer you my hand so that we could shake on such a deal but unfortunately I do not think your keepers would approve. Therefore we will settle for a verbal agreement on this matter?"

For a moment Jules hesitated but perhaps it was the thought of new found freedom that finally persuaded him to nod his acknowledgement before the prison officer opened the door which led to the cell block before the visitors were allowed to depart.

* * *

Renee Pascal breathed in the tangy air that had been infiltrated with the odour from the pounding ocean as the ferry boat nudged its way from those white cliffs of England and out into the channel. For to him it was indeed a pleasure to watch as the landmass of the country every true Frenchman both loved and hated slowly faded into the background and not for the first time he felt glad that he had chosen this way of returning to his beloved France rather than taking the shuttle from Ashburton. For this truly gave one the feeling of putting distance away from the land which had served to give the French many a headache in the past. Besides travelling by sea gave one the opportunity to think and at this time Renee Pascal was musing on the money which Stuart Bardon owed him and he wondered whether the man would be actually willing to now pay his debts.

But then of course Renee Pascal was no mug and he had dealt with such misfits before. That was why he had demanded half of the payment for his services in advance and now he had completed his task he desired the rest of the amount owed to him. Renee touched his pocket with a half-smile for inside he now had on his person the address of someone he would contact concerning Stuart Bardon's present whereabouts if the money was not forthcoming. Come to think of it he might even be tempted to contact them whether he received his payment or not for as a true Frenchman he had little time for the English particularly those who chose not only to reside on his own soil in France but who were also willing to cheat their kith and kin out of monetary gain..

As for that other Frenchman, the one who was presently languishing behind bars in an English prison well he had done his best to set the wheels in motion to spring him and therefore he now considered that he had done quite enough to complete the task that had been set for him.

Thus Renee Pascal took in deep breaths which the ozone from the ocean provided and eagerly awaited the approach of the shores of his beloved native France!

⋆ ⋆ ⋆

But please tell me, if she is not here then where is she?" The distraught young man who presented himself on the doorstep of Elaine Taylor's home gave one the impression that the he had been running for some time if his shortness of breath was anything to go by. Not that his appearance did much to enchant the likes of Elaine Taylor for such folk arriving in apparently such disarray did little to maintain the strata of society which she herself coveted and who much preferred life to be a little more predictable.

"If you are referring to Jayne then I can categorically tell you that the girl is not here. Furthermore I consider that as the two of you chose to get married then it must have been damned right careless of you to have gone and misplaced her!" She watched as her visitor began to squirm under her onslaught and breathed a sigh of relief for she considered that people should not take her good graces for granted and furthermore in her eyes this young man had a great deal to answer for.

"I can assure you that I left Jayne at the Manor whilst I had to attend to some business. When I returned Mrs Bentham, my housekeeper, informed me that my wife received a phone call which Mrs Bentham understood was from you! Indeed Mrs Bentham said that Jayne then told her that she had to come back to Esprick urgently, for something was wrong at the family home!"

"I can assure you that no such phone call came from this house!" At least Elaine Taylor's eyes had now softened as a certain hint of worry had begun to creep into them. "Why should anyone from here have phoned Jayne, for as far as I am aware there was no such problem?" It was then that Elaine Taylor appeared to have another thought, one might have decreed was uncharacteristic of her, but then the same morning she herself had received a letter from the bank stating in no uncertain terms that her own and her husband's investments could no longer be considered to be a viable proposition and therefore if this young man was reputed to have money then he might well be one to be cultivated. "Perhaps you had better come in!"

Once inside the domain Elaine Taylor became adept at showing at least some small vestige of charity. "Have you tried elsewhere? Has Jayne got her mobile with her?"

"If she does have her mobile with her then I am afraid that I am getting no response. No I didn't try elsewhere to find her for the message seemed to be quite specific, that she had come back home for some reason. And just in case you ask, there were no differences between us!"

Elaine Taylor resorted to what she always did in such a fraught situation; she immediately put the kettle on. Doing this task she believed gave her time to think and with Luc Matthieu finally settled in her kitchen drinking a mug of hot tea despite his protests, some inspiration did finally come into her head, although why this had been brought about by musing over the demise of Simon Turnbill she had no idea.

"Have you informed the authorities over her disappearance yet?"

The question almost succeeded in choking Luc who was in the process of trying to swallow a mouthful of that hot tea. "Well no, my understanding was simply that Jayne had decided to come back home after receiving a phone call!"

"Then perhaps you ought to inform them now!" With no more ado Elaine Taylor stretched to pass him the telephone although by this time Luc had already retrieved his mobile from his pocket, searching upon it for texts or messages and phoning Jayne's number yet again without boasting of any luck in being able to reach her.

It was then and after looking Elaine Taylor firmly in the eye that Luc focussed his attention on the telephone number of Detective Inspector Bennett still included on the list within his directory. To his mind, Jayne appeared to have disappeared in the South of England and therefore there seemed little point in informing the local Northern constabulary of her disappearance.

Perhaps he was indeed fortunate enough that Detective Inspector Bennett was currently at the station in Dover and even more fortunate that his desk sergeant took the urgency of Luc's appeal seriously.

"So where are you now?" The Inspector's dulcet tones appeared to roll along whatever connection they had: And then after a moment's explanation from Luc. "Then as your wife seems to have disappeared in the South of the country, might one ask what you are doing there?"

"I thought and indeed Mrs Bentham gave me to understand that Jayne had been called to go to her parents' house urgently. That is why I am here!"

"In that case I would advise you to return back to Priory Manor immediately then at least we will know where to find you should we have some news of your wife's whereabouts!" The phone call ended abruptly for the Inspector was a man not given to the over-elaboration of words and Luc was left to look at Elaine Taylor rather apologetically.

"He is right of course!" Even the rendering from a mobile had not stopped the ears of Elaine Taylor from catching its message. Indeed in one sense the woman reminded him of some Bassett hound with its ears alert to catch some snippet of information. But then perhaps he was being a little unfair on her but he had not even the opportunity to show this when the demanding voice echoed yet again "You have your car here I suppose?" And then when he nodded certainly not at that time ascertaining to what the woman was inferring. "In that case I think I had better come along with you. After all it is my daughter whom we are talking about!"

Luc blinked his eyes rather rapidly for surely this was not something that he had envisaged. On the other hand the woman was perfectly right in showing concern for her daughter and therefore for this reason and possibly because he could think up no excuse, he nodded his agreement.

Jayne tried her best to wriggle her head in an attempt to see her way out of the ghastly position she now found herself in. It was of course a natural reaction upon just regaining consciousness, but one which proved to be of no practical use whatsoever. Bound hand and foot with a gag firmly placed around her mouth she had literally only her eyes to now ascertain why she was being jostled from side to side in this manner, yet the dimness of any available light made this option only a vague hope.

As it was she tried to remember how she had managed to arrive in this position. She remembered setting out from Priory Manor only taking the second best car less her husband had need of the other and setting out to travel post haste to see what the matter was that appeared to have affected her parents so much. After receiving the phone call she supposed she had been in too much of a hurry to leave a message for Luc who was out at the time, although she knew full well that Mrs Bentham would inform him what had happened and she had determined that she would ring him just as soon as she reached Esprick.

Yet the journey had however not gone too well. Perhaps it was her own fault for taking the car that was second in line and expecting it to perform well on such a long journey. The fact that it was not however soon became apparent for even before she reached the Dartford crossing the engine had spluttered and finally had come to a stop although fortunately at the time, realising something was wrong with the vehicle she had managed to steer the vehicle off the main M25 and onto a side road.

She had in effect just reached into her handbag for her mobile to summon help when another vehicle had drawn up besides her and the driver had alighted signifying that he wanted to help. Perhaps her first mistake had been in not making that phone call for far from the help she had expected Jayne had suddenly felt herself accosted, her handbag and its contents wrested from her grip and she herself had been forced by the driver and another individual into the back seat of the car which she initially believed had come to her aid. She remembered a cloth containing some foul smelling substance being placed over her face and that was when she had lost consciousness.

Now she appeared to have returned back to the living only to find herself in this position almost indeed as if she had been placed in a wooden coffin and was now being jostled up and down on the way to her own burial. She could not shout for help because of the gag upon her lips. She could not move her limbs because of the bonds that bound them. All she had in her possession was now her eyes and enclosed in the darkness of this wooden tomb they were of little use to her either. Perhaps indeed this was exactly what it was, a living tomb, and perhaps indeed the fates looked kindly upon her as she slumped back again into an unconscious state.

For his part Luc was far too tied up to notice the antics of the two women once they arrived back at Priory Manor for to start with the two seemed to prowl around each other like two feline cats as if determined that the other would in no way gain any advantage over them. To start with Mrs Bentham was left to wonder who this creature was that the master had taken upon himself to bring back to the Hall. She knew of course that the master was upset at the disappearance of his bride, but what bringing this woman here had got to do with that matter she could not put forward any supposition. Besides Mrs Bentham objected most strongly to woman of that age being given free leave of her kitchen and this one looked as if she was someone who was deliberately searching for matters that she had neglected.

Elaine Taylor however viewed the matter a little differently, for as she had arrived at the property escorted by the new owner himself then she firmly believed in her own heart that the servant woman should at least show her a little respect.

For his part Luc sighed for surely this situation was something he could have well done without. The whole crux of the matter rested around the fact that Jayne was missing and not the adoration of two females who should have known better.

"Look, can you two please cool it? Elaine came down from Esprick with me because naturally enough she is worried about her daughter. Have we had any news on that score Mrs Bentham?"

"Not to my knowledge although come to think of it that Inspector did call with the news that your wife's car has been found although unfortunately the girl was not inside of it at the time! I suppose that stands to sense for if she had been inside of the car then folk would no longer be looking for her!"

"What my poor baby, what can have happened to her?" Upon this Luc had half expected to see the ritual of Elaine wringing her hands amidst her desperate tones, but if that was what he was waiting for then he was doomed to be disappointed for the woman appeared all the more eager to get going in an attempt to find her daughter.

"I will phone the Inspector for myself!" Luc made the decision as if he half expected the likes of these two women to have destroyed any evidence and what the Inspector wished to reveal would be lost for ever.

"I really can't say that I have ever liked that man!" Mrs Bentham determined that at least her opinion would be heard.

"And why not? How dare you come out with such a comment anyway? At least this policeman you speak about appears to have Jayne's interests at heart! Surely you must ring the man Luc and find out what he has to say!"

"Well at least one female now appears to be talking sense!" Luc turned in Elaine's direction much to the agitation of Mrs Bentham who then removed the pots from the table setting them down with a hefty bump in the kitchen which convinced the others she must have had some breakages in this act. Still Luc determined to act upon his convictions. Perhaps he was indeed lucky to find the Inspector at the station at this hour for most sane minded individuals would have long since left the fold for their underlings to manage. But then the Inspector lived and breathed his police work, many would have said to the ruin of any outside life, and at this moment in time it was a young woman he knew quite well who had disappeared.

"We have managed to trace the car, just this side of the Dartforth crossing. Apart from the fact that some little attention was required to the engine and the doors had all been left wide open no further damage has accrued to the vehicle. Of its occupant however I am afraid we have found no sign. Neither did there appear to be any sign of violence at the scene. The steering wheel however has revealed two sets of finger prints for us one of which most probably belongs to your wife. Are you still there Mr Matthieu?"

"I am still here Inspector. Indeed I am reticent to go anywhere until my wife is found!" Luc wondered where his voice came from. It did not sound like his own but rather one that was in danger of breaking up.

"Then perhaps you will be good enough to come to the depot and identify the vehicle for we have had the vehicle brought back again to Dover." Luc placed his hand over the receiver. For starters he did not want Elaine to hear any of this rhetoric, for if she did then he surely knew what would immediately follow and this was a matter that he preferred to attend to solo.

"I need to pop out for a moment!" He had spied his opportunity when the two women appeared to be busy if only eyeing up the others' talents. Indeed Elaine appeared to have forgotten all about the phone call whilst in the throes of criticising Mrs Bentham's pastry. And having made good his escape Luc held a certain feeling of pride for no one but no one had ever thought to mention the second role the townsfolk would be playing in this festival!

Still bound and finding it difficult to breathe in what appeared to be her coffin, Jayne roused suddenly as the container she was travelling in appeared to be bumping along some track rather than a road. Yet even from her confinement she heard the squeal of brakes as the whole encasement seemed to lurch forward. She thought that she heard voices yet they appeared to be coming from a distance away and she tried to struggle with her gag in an attempt to make people hear her and learn of her predicament. The vehicle lurched forward yet again and this time before she finally passed out yet again she was conscious that she had bumped her head on the side of something. After that it was sheer oblivion and whatever happened next passed over her in her unconscious state.

It was Detective Inspector Bennett who finally took the message at the station. At the time he was on his own with one rather distraught husband who had already identified the vehicle that had been found as his and who had claimed that this was indeed the same vehicle that Jayne had commenced her journey in that day.

"We have some news!" The Inspector looked stern as he confronted the young man. "It appears that we have managed to apprehend a goods vehicle down at the docks apparently in the process of attempting to gain passage to France. The security guys down at the port are to be commended, for bearing in mind my previous theory they embarked upon a thorough search of the vessel, a process which would hardly have been conducted in normal conditions. As a result of their endeavours a girl was found trussed up in no uncertain manner in the interior of that vehicle and what is more we have reason to believe that this could be your missing wife!"

"What!" Luc stood ready now to make his exit to the port.

"A moment please Mr Matthieu. First of all when found the girl was unconscious. Indeed in the confines where she was being kept then she is indeed lucky to be alive. My colleagues naturally phoned for the ambulance to have the girl taken to hospital before continuing with their line of enquiries!"

"Then I must go to her!" Luc thought no more about Jayne's abductors his sole intention now to be back with his wife.

"At the moment I must warn you that the girl is still unconscious for as well as being kept in the most ridiculous conditions confined bound and gagged in a coffin like container she also appears to have banged her head on her surrounds, possibly when the vehicle was stopped. Nevertheless the first prognosis on her condition is that she should be all right given time to recover from her appalling confinement as well as the injuries sustained. Maybe it is as well that her confinement in that transporter was not of an over long duration!"

"But I can still go to her?"

"Of course just so long as you understand the situation and do not expect too much response from the girl at this time. Indeed the hospital will welcome your identification. I myself will be joining my colleagues down at the port for the people in charge of this transporter will obviously have questions to answer! Having said that I myself will wish to see your wife once she ahs recovered consciousness"

Luc waited to hear no more and was out through the door almost before the Inspector had finished what he was saying leaving the other with a grim smile about his lips. But there again, the Inspector concluded, if things had happened in reverse, would he have acted any differently to Luc Matthieu?

It was the following day before Jayne finally regained consciousness. At first, finding herself in a hospital bed the reality of the situation was difficult for her to comprehend even though a flash back from the past alerted her senses to the bonds which had held her fast and the horrendous situation she had found herself in. How she had now come to be in this place apparently attached to a drip, she had no idea although as her eyes took in her new surrounds she recognised the figure of her husband who was currently gazing down at her a worried expression in his eyes.

"Don't worry, everything is all right!" He had noticed the slight flickering of her eye lashes as she began to regain consciousness and the fact was whether he himself considered matters to be all right could be held in scant regard as he tried to comfort his wife.

She opened her mouth to try to say something to him but any words she might have uttered were interrupted by the arrival of that starched white uniform as the ward sister decided to see how her patient was faring. "Ah you are back with us Mrs Matthieu; that is good. But you must now try to relax and try not to dwell on things that have happened in the past. There will be time enough for you to remember those once you are stronger!" The woman held out some water for her to suck through a pipette and then perhaps decided to mention Luc almost as if he was an afterthought

"Your husband is here Mrs Matthieu. He may stay for a while on the understanding that he does not upset you with reference to the past at this moment. Not that is until you are stronger and such memories have no repercussions on you. The doctor has examined you and you have no need to worry for there is no lasting damage done, you are suffering from dehydration which is why you are attached to a drip at the moment but that is only a temporary measure. The doctor did say however that any visitors at this time must be kept to a minimum. That is why we decided that perhaps your husband was the one best qualified to sit by your bedside and indeed the only visitor!"

The ward sister moved away now having contented herself that she had done right by her patient. Not that Jayne, now awakened had any intention of leaving it to the future to fill the gaps in her present knowledge and she turned to the one who held her hand questions urging themselves forward from out of her lips.

"You heard what the sister said. You have to rest!" Still Luc knew full well that the girl would not rest, not at least until she had acquired some basic knowledge of what had befallen her and he sighed for with Jayne in a mood like that there was little he could do but to admit at least in part some of the things which had brought her to this place. "Do you remember nothing?"

Luc thought he saw Jayne wracking her brains before she finally shook her head. "Fortunately on Detective Inspector Bennett's instigation a heavy goods vehicle was stopped as it left the holding compound to board the ferry boat to France and upon searching the thing the officers eventually found you in the act of being transported across the channel bound within a container that resembled a coffin!"

Memories slowly began flooding back to her as she shivered. "It was not very comfortable in that tomb I admit. I thought I was no longer able to breathe whilst the stench around was pretty horrible!"

"You bumped your head on that container when the vehicle was finally stopped and that was what knocked you out cold!"

Fleetingly the memories began to return but then Jayne wanted to find out more. "The car started to act up, I thought that they had stopped to help but instead they bound and gagged me and placed me in that horrible place; but why?"

"Perhaps at the moment it might be as well not to dwell on such matters!" He could see by her eyes that she was ready to lapse back into a sleep so he sat there in silence merely holding her hand.

"Maybe you would be far more comfortable if you got a good night's rest Mr Matthieu!" The sister had returned and noticing that Jayne was once more asleep and the hours of visiting had long since past, probably desired to have the ward once more to herself but Luc shook his head.

"I will stay here less she wakens again. Besides it is probably far more peaceful here than being confined to a house with two females who by this time must surely have declared war on one another!"

The sister smiled but she did not order him off the premises so instead Luc spent the night in the chair by Jayne's bedside listening to her breathe quite easily now and offering a prayer of thanks that she was well on the way to recovery.

The hospital authorities decided to keep Jayne for an extra day in view of the concussion she had suffered although as she was now able to drink and feed herself the drip was removed. Feeling the threat of two certain ladies arriving to see what was going on, Luc took the opportunity to phone them and to say that Jayne was all right. That was a task easier said than done as far as her mother was concerned, for the woman immediately thought she would have a beneficial role to play at the hospital until Luc fabricated the truth a little by saying that at the moment she was not allowed any visitors.

"Visitors? But I am not a visitor. I am the girl's mother!"

"And I Elaine happen to be her husband and only I have a concession to stay here!"

Jayne smiled her thanks when Luc told her for in all truth the thought of her mother around the hospital at this time did little for her. It was during the afternoon that the Inspector arrived having inquired at the relevant places whether he could interview the girl and Luc found himself having somewhat unwillingly to agree with this visit. Still he had to admit that the man had a smile on his face when he came into the ward.

"I am the bearer of some news for you!" In truth the Detective seemed ready to make himself at home once he had established that Jayne was now none the worse for her ordeal.

"The two men who subjected you to this rather vicious attack have now been apprehended and indeed once charged they were obviously ready to comment on who had employed them. As a result I have been in touch with the French police and as a result I must inform you Mr Matthieu that one of your British relatives has now been apprehended, a Mr Stuart Bardon by name. From the evidence we have received so far it would appear that this man, currently residing in France, was the instigator of many of your problems for it appeared that he believed himself to be in the position to be able to hire underlings to complete his dirty work for him: The fact that it was an Englishman who was behind this arena of deception appeared also to please the French police. Therefore I do not envisage that you will find him being of much trouble to you in the near future!"

Luc gripped Jayne's hand tightly. At first perhaps she had expected to see a glimmer of regret in Luc's eyes that Stuart Bardon who happened to be related to him was currently due to experience the full displeasure of the law, but Luc exhibited none of this. How indeed could he after the man in question had treated him so?

"I am only too pleased that the matter had finally been cleared up Inspector. Not only for my own sake but also for Jayne's for how could my wife have possibly been content if such villains had been allowed to roam free?"

Perhaps the Inspector saw something in the couple's eyes that made him feel that perhaps he was now overstaying his welcome, for shortly afterwards he made his excuses to leave a feeling of peace descending over the couple. They had much to talk about but such talk did not include any relative of Luc Matthieu

Jayne was allowed home the next day after satisfying the doctors that she had now fully recovered from her traumatic experience and it was only as the pair journeyed back to the Manor that they remembered what would be awaiting them. Yet instead of the wholesale war that both of them were convinced must have broken out between the two women a certain ethos of calm appeared to have enveloped the place with both women now apparently content to work side by side without the triads of the past.

Yet as far as Elaine Taylor was concerned Luc had now something to say to the woman who in truth had only her daughter's interests at heart.

"Mam, you don't mind if I call you that do you?" And when Elaine shook her head still mystified at what was to follow. "The thing is Jayne and I are going to be fully occupied in this region bringing this place up to standard, a place fit to live in and less of a Mausoleum. With this in mind I was wondering if you and Mr Taylor would take charge of the land and its subsequent development near to your home. Maybe something will come out of the shale gas project, maybe not, but the land will still be there to be used at your own jurisdiction. Can I ask if you will do this as a favour for me?"

Elaine Taylor opened and closed her mouth for several seconds before a positive sound issued forth. Jayne in fact had never seen her parent so speechless before and regarded it as a great novelty. "Good with your agreement I will see my solicitor and draw up the necessary papers even before you return to Esprick for I have every confidence in both you and your husband becoming the legal guardians of that property: And now you have both established that my wife id perfectly all right and none the worse for her ordeal, we would like to spend some time together!" He took Jayne's hand with a smile and the two of them left the room together. After all there are certain things one does not always want to share with relatives, however well -meaning they might be!

Poem for Random Encounter

Travelling Incognito
When you're travelling incognito
With a special place to go
Just adopt a casual pose
And keep your head down low.
Don't voice any innuendos
Or let your temper show!
When you're travelling incognito
With a special place to go!

Other Novels by Kathleen Steele

MARINA BAIXA - Romance and Intrigue leads from the security of the Lake District to uncertainty in Spain!

ARMS OF GOLD - Following September 11th, what connection does the Lake at Windermere have with the Mediterranean around Majorca?

RADIANT VIBES - Pollution in the Irish Sea leads to strange findings and unusual relationships!

OASIS IN TIME - The location of those illusive weapons of mass destruction provides surprises!

PUT AND TAKE - Casinos on the Fylde Coast? Would you like to take a chance?

THE UPPER CUT - Scurrilous behaviour on those Upper Reaches serves to create ripples that stir those once still waters!

THE PINK ROSE - The Border Folk's response to the proposed Regional Assemblies brings mayhem!

TWO FACED - Buying a computer should require a Government Health Warning!

ROUND AND ROUND - Wind and Tide can make uneasy bedfellows in the struggle to find a new Power Source!

NEXT STOP PARADISE – Love and intrigue are stimulated on life's merry-go-round!

CHECK OUT - The development of the provincial Airport, heralds the development in human relationships

HIDE AND SEEK - Hidden treasures require attention to detail, or else!

LOST AND FOUND - Where there's a will, there's a way!

FOOTLOOSE - When a positive charge meets a positive charge, then!

IN THE SHADOW OF THE STORM - Do the fish always behave like that or is this the calm before the storm?

DISTRACTION - A hidden cell in the Lake District leads to a tempest of ferocity which contrasts sharply with the peace and tranquillity that place is noted for!

A LIGHTER SHADE OF PINK - A sequel as requested to THE PINK ROSE. Meet the various characters again as this time our friends attempt to extend their franchise into Cumbria!

THE HEART'S REFRAIN - The mists around those magical Islands reflect the mist that obscures Anton's vision.

THE TURN OF THE WHEEL - Romance and fortune can be linked!

VENGEFUL RETURN - Two men and yet there can only ever be one boat! A sequel to MARINA BAIXA and NEXTSTOP PARADISE

NOT HERE - What is the connection between that house fire and those windmills out at sea?

THE RUN OF THE RABBIT - Could the government really be conspiring to move that Nuclear Power Plant into the midst of the Langdale Valley?

STAR OF THE DAWN - Can the star of early morning point the way to life's fulfilment?

SKETCH ME LOVE - The shrouding mist of those tranquil Islands serves to disguise a more sinister scheme to involve them in man's game!

SPLIT WIDE OPEN - Mischievous Pranks or mysterious happenings disturb the peace in the hamlet of FellBeck!

POWERFUL CIRCLES - What is the connection between those ancient customs and the future?

BISPHAM BROOK - Could this be the case where such water comes to create mayhem or is there something more sinister behind the apparently innocent flow?

CRAB ISLAND - The Atlantic Isles offer peace, tranquillity and dramatic scenery to the innocent holidaymaker yet one cannot but speculate that there is something more!

SHAP - The fells of North West England may provide a refuge but other things also transpire in a community that proves that they are not quite so isolated!

INNER TURMOIL - Recovering from a trauma in her life Krisha is soon to find that the past often has a habit of catching up on one!

CRISP LIES THE TRACK - Will the ashes of the past support the love of today?

THE VIPER'S BITE - Beware of reptiles with warm blood in their veins!

SOFTLY THE NIGHT - Rags to riches perhaps?

VEIL OF SECRETS - Can love survive the tide of deception?

WEB OF TORMENT - When the storm infiltrates, can peace survive?

STRICTURES OF THE HEART - Eruption serves to spark the heart.

ECHOES FROM THE PAST - Harmony sounds a discordant note.

A NATURAL CHOICE - Water water everywhere, be careful where you step.

AN UNEVEN STEP - Can the murderer be found in the most unlikely of circumstances?

THE CURTAIN RISES - When evil strikes, can love prevail?

TIME STOOD STILL - Will time reveal its hidden secrets?

HIGHWAY TO LOVE - Can fortune's treasures find true love?

HEADING INTO INTRIQUE - When the door closes can love survive?

A HEART IN TURMOIL - When flares abide can love be blind?

BOUND BY LOVE - Look up at the stars instead of the earth

THE THREAD THAT BINDS US - Seen in the dusk, gone by the dawn, can ancient sagas be believed?

RANDOM ENCOUNTER - Can time be dependent upon the weapons of power?

If you have difficulty in obtaining any of
the above copies contact 01253 591905